of

Jaded Justice

Author:

R. L. Dodson

Dedicated to

My Father

The past is lost in a sea of darkness forever and the future is but a faint glimpse on the horizon.

R L Dodson

Heart of Jaded Justice

Heart of

Jaded Justice

Heart of Jaded Justice

R. L. Dodson

Copyright 2013 by R L Dodson

All rights reserved.

ISBN-13: 978-1482580679

ISBN-10: 1482580675

This book is a work of fiction. Names, characters, places and incidents are either the product of the author's imagination or are used fictitiously. Any resemblances to actual events, locales, or persons, living or dead are entirely coincidental.

Cover Design by: Regina McDonald and R. L. Dodson

PROLOGUE

Bay City, Florida

12:48 A.M.

The torrential rain was unrelenting, whipped into a frenzy by hurricane force winds, and the waves surged and crashed against the coast, a bedlam in the dark night. The freak storm would catch the mark unawares but was good; it provided better cover than they could have hoped for.

From the beach, a sliver of blue light flickered on and off four times, a signal from the SWAT team that it was safe to proceed. Safe! What did that mean? Experience as a teacher, nothing was ever really safe. Ashley leaned against the dark confines of the speeding machine, her heart racing wildly with adrenaline. She glared out the dark tinted windows and tried to survey the passing geography to no avail as the windows were too dark and the weather too bad for anything to be visible to the naked eye. Ashley was suddenly lurched forward as the van made an immediate halt. The night air was uncomfortably hot and humid in spite of the rain beating down, as the task force team exited the black surveillance van. They were close enough to the ocean to get a whiff of salty sea air, and hear the surf pounding the shore. Each agent rushed forward toward their assigned location. This felon was like Houdini, he always managed to escape. Ricky Martinelli was about to be apprehended, one of many subjected to the round-up they were doing in culmination of "Operation Sunburn." He was the son of a Colombian Drug Lord. One responsible for sole-handedly filling the streets of the emerald coast with more cocaine and heroin than all of the other drug smugglers combined. This one night was the end of two years of exhaustive and deep undercover work.

Ashley was so anxious; her veins coursed with adrenalin as she was the first to arrive at the entrance to the Estate, equipped with certified copies of arrest and search warrants. She was assigned to lead the team bringing in Martinelli, other teams were spread out over four counties throughout the panhandle area. They were using the RICO Act. Under the RICO Act, a person could be charged with racketeering — which included bribery, extortion, illegal drug sales, loan sharking, murder and prostitution — if he or she had committed two of the 27 federal and eight state crimes under U.S. legislation, within a 10-year period. The law gives the government the power to criminally prosecute and imprison an organized crime leader even if they had never personally committed any of the components of racketeering. Reason being, he or she is part of a criminal enterprise. Ricardo "Ricky" Martinelli was part of the criminal enterprise of the Martinelli Colombian Drug Cartel and was well over the two of twenty seven federal and eight state crimes necessary. They had all the signed witness affidavits to prove the elements statutorily required, however, it would cost the government immensely in relocation and Witness Protection fees.

On the shore, the team leader who had flashed the blue signal was barking orders with unquestioned authority. Removing their black rubber dry suits to reveal dark clothing and blackened faces, they extracted their weapons from their SWAT bags and began distributing their arsenal of sub machine guns, sniper rifles and night vision goggles. Suddenly the beach was flooded with bright light. The SWAT team leader turned and realized they were surrounded and vastly outnumbered by dozens of Drug Cartel Henchmen. Bursts of automatic gunfire hit the SWAT team men. Their blood curdling screams were silenced by the fierceness of the storm, as their bodies toppled to the ground in awkward positions. The blood from their lifeless bodies washing out to sea.

Meanwhile, additional DEA Task Force members had flooded the exterior of the estate grounds and were surrounding it; canvassing and assessing potential exits, should Ricky Martinelli decide to flee.

"Don't open the door, Ashley." Tony screamed from the back courtyard area of the estate.

She had had enough of Tony ordering her around

and bitching. "Just shut up and stop acting like a hard ass."

Ashley scowled across the huge expanse of lawn toward Tony, shooting rain biting at her face. He didn't look as if he wanted to cooperate. He looked more like a man approaching a deadly situation as he covered the acre grounds that separated them. With one coordinated movement Ashley peeled back the hood of her rain jacket and clamored silently up the steps, hammering on the massive oak door above which hung a wooden sign hanging by solid gold entwined rings. Scrawled in fine black cursive writing burnt into the sign was the address they all knew too well; "1096 Pineview Lane - Martinelli Estate." The huge estate sat in the middle of ten acres surrounded by iron fencing.

"Drug Enforcement Administration, open the door!" Ashley announced before banging on the massive door once again.

"Don't open the door, it's going to blow!" Tony screamed at Ashley as he ran across the large expanse of lawn.

Ashley couldn't decipher what Tony was saying as he was too far away and what sounded like a loud generator kicked on from inside the estate. A commotion immediately outside the front door drew her attention momentarily as she reached down and pushed the cold brass handle down to release the latch on the front door. She heard the whipping sound of propellers coming from overhead. "Damn, it was a chopper on the roof; Martinelli was probably getting away, again. Where the hell was the SWAT Team coming in from the beach?"

Ashley stepped into the home and called up the ornate mahogany spiral staircase for Ricky Martinelli to present himself.

Ashley heard Tony screaming, "Get the hell out of there, now!" Thunder and lightning crackled in the air.

Ashley immediately smelled an extremely strong cordite (gunpowder), tritonal (TNT) and hot metal combination; when suddenly the massive estate began crackling like rockets exploding. Shards of glass from the windows were flying everywhere as the elegant chandelier came crashing downward. Wood splinters were flying and fires were breaking out as a sharp object lodged itself into the side of her neck. Pain like molten hot lava shot down her spine before the buzzing started in her ears. The buzz became louder and louder........

Ashley saw a staircase piece become an instant projectile and slice through the chest of one of the agents, blood was oozing everywhere.

She crawled toward him to try and help him but it was too late. Ashley began to make her way to what was once the front door; she heard an agonizing scream from another agent whom the chandelier had almost completely decapitated. Smoke was filling the air and fire was beginning to consume everything.

"Ashley, Ashley......" she could hear Tony calling her name from far away.

The buzzing became louder and louder and darkness began to descend upon her. One last glimpse before she succumbed to total darkness was Tony's face and his long flowing dark hair; leaning over her bloodstained body, calling her name over and over.........

Ashley screamed and bolted upright in bed. She

was covered in perspiration and her breath was coming in gasps as she felt her face, her hands, and her body. She was alive. She looked over at the clock on her nightstand, 12:48 in red digital numbers. Almost 1:00 A.M., damn.

"Momma, are you okay?" A. J. appeared at the foot of her bed with tears brimming in his eyes.

"Yes, honey. Mommy just had a bad dream. Come on and I will tuck you back in your bed." Ashley regained her composure, slipped out of bed, pulled on her robe and went down the hallway to put her son back to bed. Her dream was so vivid this time even the time was the same. She could actually smell the aftermath of the bomb, pungent gunpowder, burnt flesh and simply put; the bloody smell of death.

Ashley read her son his favorite bedtime story about Dinosaurs and he quickly drifted back off to sleep as she gently brushed the hair from his forehead and brushed her lips across his cheek. She had immersed herself in her work and her son in order to delete the reoccurring nightmares but had failed miserably. She'd prayed she would find a way to banish those fears for good and just live a normal life.

The ringing of the phone had her rushing back down the hall to catch the noise maker before A. J. was awakened for the second time in one night.

"Hello." Ashley answered a little out of breath.

"Ash are you okay, you don't sound good. This is Uncle Morgan."

"Just another nightmare, I thought they would have stopped after so many years. What is wrong for you to call this late or should I say early morning hour?" Ashley quickly deduced that something was wrong with her uncle.

"I need to come over right away, something terrible has happened." Uncle Morgan's voice cracked.

"I will go downstairs and start a pot of coffee. The door will be open." Ashley laid the receiver back in its cradle and checked in on A. J. before descending the stairs to the kitchen.

Ashley glanced nervously through the bay windows in the kitchen as the coffee brewed. She noted the almost full moon casting its soft glow against the clouds and stars in a mystical manner. Ashley wondered what troubles brewed on the horizon tonight; it had to be very important for Uncle Morgan to contact her at this hour.

Uncle Morgan and Aunt Lynn were almost the only family she had left which was the reason she had moved to D.C. five years earlier. Uncle Morgan was the Governor of D.C. and had assisted her in starting up her own business. He and Aunt Lynn had one son, Patrick who was now twenty three years old and adored her son, A. J. Her best friend Gina Rae and her husband Larry lived in D.C. as well. Gina Rae had been her rock during the deep undercover operations she had worked over the years and now they all ran Ashley's business. Larry, a retired cop was her Chief Investigator. They had all worked together for many years and were very close. Gina Rae remembered the years well; getting 2 a.m. phone calls from Ashley, just so she could touch base with reality when she had been undercover for too long.

Heart of Jaded Justice

CHAPTER ONE

The sky was turning a dull golden red by the time the plane from Washington, D.C. landed at the Florida International Airport. Chase Brady glanced at the dial of his Rolex watch, sighing with relief at the arrival of the D.C. flight which was over two hours late. He had been nervous and anxious since Ashley's three a.m. phone call yesterday morning, when she had told him in an almost frantic state that she would be arriving back in Florida. Chase had worked with the Drug Enforcement Administration for 16 years now, so three a.m. calls were not unheard of; as a matter of fact they were the more subdued events of his nocturnal life.

But this call was entirely a different matter; Ashley was his best friend, his soul mate as far as friends were concerned. She had spent 12 years working narcotics before leaving the administration early to retire in D.C. Something was terribly amiss, for her to return to Florida. They had forged a bond of friendship over the years which had remained strictly platonic.

She was like a sister, a member of his family; and she and his wife were good friends.

Just as the hustle and bustle of the embarking tourists started to fade, Chase looked out the windows and saw her exiting the plane. All 5'10" inches of her, clad in nothing other than jeans and a D.C. Sweatshirt, long raven dark hair cascading down her shoulders and tangling around the black sunshades she wore. Ashley appeared much thinner than the last time they had visited her in D.C., back in the spring. They talked frequently but visits had become seldom as they both had very hectic work schedules. He was proud of her accomplishments. Ashley was the sole owner of Cameron Private Investigations Agency. She primarily did background investigations for large corporate agencies, and overseas governmental contractors; avoiding criminal work as much as possible, which he understood considering Ashley had been beaten and left for dead when undercover cops had burnt her resulting in two contract hits on her life. She had never understood how the Dixie Mafia had managed to buy off what she thought were good cops. Not to mention the bloodbath of the last major operation they had worked together. Chase couldn't help but wonder what she might have come across that would make her return to Florida. She had sworn she would never come back for personal reasons.

Ashley Cameron glanced nervously around the volume of tourists filling the Airport. The flight had been delayed due to the massive amount of snow the unexpected late morning blizzard had dumped. The snow should have been gone by this time of year. She knew that no matter how off schedule her flight might have been, Chase would be waiting. Ashley shielded her eyes to the faint stream of sunlight filtering through the clouds above as she descended the short flight of stairs leading to the asphalt runway and made her way inside the airport terminal. She scanned the crowd looking for the 6"4" inch frame of Chase. He had such a striking appearance, he couldn't be missed; with his long hair, beard and mustache. He had often been compared to "Grizzly Adams", but very few people knew he was just a huge teddy bear. Ashley cherished her most valuable friend in the whole world. Chase knew everything about her and they had always been there for each other, always had each other's backs. She was sure he was puzzled that she was back in Florida after five years.

Numerous times during the flight she had questioned her sanity at returning to the location of such painful memories. This place had devoured her soul. But, considering the outcome of the meeting at the Governor's Office the night before, she was left with absolutely no alternative. If only she didn't have so many unresolved feelings, this trip would not feel like she was headed to the death chamber. Quite the opposite to be exact, she had left a lot of very dear friends in Bay City which was a small gulf side town in Northern Florida.

"Hello Beautiful Lady!" Chase called out across the airport lobby.

Ashley Cameron ran across the lobby to be engulfed in a bear hug so tight she could hardly breathe.

"Thanks for coming on such short notice; I knew you would. I booked the reservation yesterday morning and had a straight flight. I arrived early because I had checked baggage with my firearms and had to declare them with the agent at check-in. You can't fly with loaded clips anymore either, so I just lost four clips of ammo." replied Ashley.

"I checked the terminal gate earlier, so I knew you were delayed in D.C. and then Atlanta. There is nothing like losing six or eight hours out of your day due to airport screw ups. I have very seldom flown anywhere in the states without a layover or two of some kind. I'll send someone to collect your luggage, right now let's find some place in the shade and have a cool one so you can explain what this is all about." Chase put his arm around Ashley's shoulders and ushered her out of the airport lobby into the green Jaguar double parked outside.

Neither of them noticed the three gentlemen that exited the airport behind them or the black Lincoln with dark tinted windows that was following their progress onto the Interstate ramp. Chase was listening as Ashley filled him in briefly on the problem at hand. The trio continued following them at a safe distance, until they exited at the Bay City.

"Bay City doesn't appear to have changed a lot in five years", commented Ashley as they neared the docks. Several pelicans took flight into the red gold evening sunset as the jaguar approached. Only a few couples were milling around the port as the boats docked there, swished up and down against the tide. Even the sunset did little to diminish the humid heat from the air, in total contrast to the cooler weather she had just left in D.C. She took a deep breath, inhaling the fragrant salty sea air, the exhilarating scent refreshing her exhausted body.

"More changes than you'd care to know about, doll." Chase murmured as he exited the Jaguar, motioning for Ashley to join him down the gangplanks leading to a fifty six foot cabin cruiser.

"What is this monstrous vessel?" she asked.

"This baby belongs to me; you can hang out here while you are in town. I hate to run but the District Attorney is waiting for a report I have to get in and I have to get a few depositions in order for trial tomorrow; he called and there is a problem I have to take care of immediately; so our cool drink will have to wait. You have my cell number, if you need anything. I'll hook up with you around midnight tonight, and you can fill me in on all the details." Chase kissed Ashley on the cheek as he dropped the keys to the cabin door in her hand.

"Pete, one of my men; will pick up your luggage from the airport and be along shortly to drop it off. I have already told him to provide you with some ammo. He has an arsenal in his SUV, just tell him what you need for your weapons."

"Thanks again, Chase; I'll explain everything to you in detail tonight. Right now I just want a warm bath and try to sort through some relevant case files I brought along with me. I have my cell phone with me, and my .357 and .45 will be in my luggage when your man gets it here. Although I hope I don't have to shoot anyone before you get back. Besides, if I empty my guns at anything - I will just throw the darn things at them and run!" Ashley laughingly hugged Chase and waved him off the boat.

Chase drove away from the docks, noting the D.C. plates on the black Lincoln as he passed the exit sign out of the dock area. The car was parked inconspicuously enough, but some gut feeling made Chase check the plates, probably no coincidence that the D.C. plates were in the dock area just as Ashley had flown in from D.C. The windows of the Lincoln were darkened so it was impossible for him to get a look at the occupants. What had Ashley gotten herself into now? He circled back around and found nothing suspicious enough about the vehicle to warrant a search. He would still have the Police Department run a check on the plates just to be safe, Chase reached for the police radio concealed in the glove compartment, and entered the ramp back onto the interstate heading toward the Courthouse in the downtown district. He called the information in and waited and waited. After 10 minutes he simply threw the walkie back into the glove compartment, after uttering several profane statements about the capabilities of the local police department. He would check with the P.D. when he arrived back at his office.

Chase glanced at his Rolex, damn the thing, he hated watches, hated to live on a time frame for that matter. Chase entered the courthouse, whistling *As Time Goes By* from the movie Casablanca; as he walked down the corridor and entered the DA's office. "Late again as usual", barked District Attorney Steve Andrews; and "stop that infernal whistling."

DA Andrews looked down the bridge of his nose over the top of his reading glasses and stated, "Your office has left you three urgent messages in the last 15 minutes in reference to a tag you ran earlier. It came back to a stolen vehicle. I don't suppose you know where the vehicle is now by any chance, do you?"

"I called that tag in over forty minutes ago and became tired of waiting for those dim-wits to get back with me. Why the hell did they call my office, I called them on the radio and was on the radio in the car waiting for a reply!" Chase snatched the hit sheet from D.A. Andrews and yelled at him, "get some units down to the dock at Bay City. I just dropped off an ex-agent down there. She's in from D.C., which is where the vehicle was stolen."

Andy Gonzales, D.A. Investigator, rushed into the District Attorney's Office swearing and ran square into Chase. "Damn pier has been blown to smithereens down at Bay City, are you headed that way?"

Chase shouted, "Keep up if you're going with me, my Department already has units in route."

"Steve, I will explain it all later as soon as I know myself what the hell is going on. Keep radio frequencies on emergency stand-by channels." Chase called back to the D.A. as he headed out the door.

"Gonzales, come on!" Chase ordered, while shoving Gonzales through the outer door.

The Jaguar sped away from the downtown district like a flash. By the time they reached the docks, Gonzales was ashen white; while sirens blared and fire trucks flooded the area that was already filled with thick black clouds of smoke. Chase had a sick feeling in the pit of his stomach wondering if Ashley had survived the explosion. The empty sloop where his cabin cruiser had nestled mere hours earlier only deepened his anxiety. He should have stayed with her, he should have canceled the meeting with the D.A., he should have found out what was wrong, never mind that Ashley had made light of the situation, knowing her as he did that's exactly what she would do, no matter how bad.

Fire Chief Baxter assembled his men to contain the licking flames from spreading over to the adjacent port. Firemen loaded down with hoses gushing powerful bursts of water scampered along the remainder of the dock like a disturbed bed of ants. Only the slip where Chase's boat had rested was completely demolished. Scattered debris covered the water so thickly that you could not see where the dock ended and the bay water began. Within a short time the firemen had the flames under control and the fire contained to smoldering ashes.

"Chief Baxter, what do we know?" Chase extended his hand in greeting.

"Well, we are dealing with professionals and it seems as if they intended for this one port to go and that is all. An IED,

(Improvised Explosive Devise) appears to be the source. The IED has five components; the switch, initiator, container, charge and power source. We have located the switch and the power source so far. The final report will be available in the morning, detailing the type of charge used. My men are canvassing the area and collecting samples; the dive team will be here soon. They should be able to locate the pieces of the initiator and container. I don't know how much they will be able to see right now. With the sun going down; we may have to send them in again when there is enough daylight to see properly, and to allow time for some of the debris to settle. I prefer to get them here now as a "search" team and not wait until we have a "rescue" need. Remote detonation is likely; we found a garage door opener with minimal charring which could have set off the device. Detonation time could have been pre-set to anywhere from 15 minutes to an hour. Apparently there were no fatalities as the port was empty at this time of evening. What brings DEA out here, anyway?" Chief Baxter asked in puzzlement.

"I dropped off a friend about two hours ago; was sloop eight empty? Or could you tell from all the damage and debris?" Chase asked looking about at the ravages of the explosion.

"I would say that it was empty, there is a lot of debris, but it is from the dock itself. We found some casing and shrapnel at the far end of the dock. Like I said the detonation could have been remotely pre-set, which would have allowed time for the bombers to leave the area, it also allowed time for the boat to leave it appears. They must have attached the device to the dock and not the boat itself. There was very little debris in actual boat sloop vicinity and nothing indicative of boat hull, or mass. Maybe your friend went for an evening sail, we can have the marine Patrol scout the area; tell me who or what we are looking for Chase." Baxter took a pad from his pocket.

"That would be a good idea." Chase acknowledged giving the Chief a full description of the 56 foot cabin cruiser painted sky blue with *Free Bird* scrawled in black cursive lettering on both her sides. He explained to the Chief that the female friend was an ex-agent with the Drug Enforcement Administration and that it might be safer to keep her name out of the investigation for the time being. Chase headed back to the jaguar to get his cell phone. There was a chlorine chemical smell in the air which meant the bomb had a large payload with a high explosive charge more than likely. He gave one more disgusted look at the dial of his Rolex. His life had been turned upside down in just a matter of four hours. That girl could get in more trouble than anyone he had known his entire life without even trying. Ashley was like a magnet; death, trials and tribulations were just attracted to her, like they stuck to her everywhere she went. Chase yanked the Jaguar door open and reached in for the cell phone. Damn, he had eight missed calls from an unknown caller. He hoped that Ashley was the caller and that she had left a message or would keep trying until she reached him.

No messages. Chase tossed the phone back on the seat. Maybe she was okay and had removed the cruiser from the dock of her own accord and had not been kidnapped or worse killed. He was also uncertain if she could handle the cruiser alone if she had decided to take it out; as it had been at least five years since she had been on a boat of any kind much less one the size of *Free Bird*.

A gentle rapping on the window caused Chase to jump;

just as he was putting the jag in reverse.

"What's up Pete?" Chase called as the window was sliding down.

"Chase, I came by right after you left and dropped off Miss Cameron's luggage. She was okay then, said she was going to take a bath and rest. She thanked me for dropping off her luggage and a couple of file boxes. I gave her plenty of ammo for her 357 and 45 which were in her luggage. I stopped off at the sheriff's office substation and had gotten halfway back into town when I heard on the police radio about the explosion down here. The only vehicle I noticed was a black Lincoln, but I didn't get the license plates. I should have checked it out, Chase." Pete was shaking his head in sorrow.

"Don't worry about it Pete. I saw the same vehicle, pulled the plates and called them in to the P.D. They came back on a stolen vehicle, it just took them so long to give me the information that I was already back at the courthouse. We will find them, just hang out here and see what you can come up with. I will be available by radio if you have anything for me." With that Chase sped away from the dock.

As Chase headed back towards the office he was notified by dispatch that the police department had just located the stolen vehicle from D.C. and they were in a high speed pursuit as the fleeing vehicle had just entered the on ramp to the interstate at Beachfront Avenue. Chase reached in the glove compartment and took out his police microphone.

"P.D., this is Brady - Which on ramp is the D.C. stolen vehicle taking, east or west?"

"Dispatch 104 to Brady, East Ramp onto Interstate 3".

Chase tossed the microphone onto the dashboard and floored the green Jaguar as he intended to be present when they stopped these thugs. He had quite a few questions he wanted to ask them and he'd be damned but they would answer one way or the other.

CHAPTER TWO

Ashley stood at the bow of the cruiser glaring at the tremendous balls of fire hurling black smoke toward the sky. The blackened stains on the horizon looked as if a volcano had spit her molten lava skyward, burning and pulverizing everything in her path; then raining down nothing but ashes. She had heard the explosion and with a sickening realization, knew it came from the port she had departed just a mere thirty minutes earlier.

She looked out at the vast expanse of water surrounding her and felt a little safer than if she had stayed in port. Judging by the fiery clouds of smoke back at the port, she had made the right decision. She was really uncertain what had dictated the need to escape the port, other than the two body builder looking men that kept hanging around the dock, after Pete had dropped off her things. Ashley had first noticed them walking away from her cruiser, even though she had not seen them arrive. Come to think of it, she hadn't noticed them there when she and Chase had arrived. How had they managed to get to her cruiser and be leaving before she ever noticed them? She was definitely losing her edge, that and the fact that she was exhausted. The void blackness of the vast empty sea was preferable to the vapor lights and sirens illuminating Port Bay City. She desperately hoped that no one had been injured, and this deep gnawing fear that she was to blame somehow, made matters worse.

What was she to do? She had to let Chase know that she hadn't been hurt, or killed. But was her cell phone safe to use? Was the explosion intended for her? It didn't seem likely that it would be a coincidence; I mean she had just arrived at the Port. If she had not felt so uneasy and restless earlier she would have stayed at the dock. She had been cautious of the two strangers and had felt that the crisp clean salty ocean air would relax her so that she could better think and sort through the case files she had brought with her. The more she pondered the more she realized that the best avenue seemed to be to stay anchored miles from shore until sunrise and then head for another port and contact Chase from there. He would be worried but would instinctively know that she was safe. He might however, be concerned whether his little *Free Bird* was still afloat.

The full moon cast shadows across the bow as the stars twinkled like diamonds in the black velvet sky above. The salty air acted as a buffer against the acrid smoke smells drifting out across the sea. Ashley wondered how such a beautiful and serene place could once again be the stage of another violent assault. She had this gut feeling that a terrorist action of some kind was what had just occurred back at the port, and she had definitely learned over the years to trust that gnawing gut feeling. The balls of fire and the thunderous sound of the explosion earlier had left her quite disoriented.

The rumbling in her stomach reminded her that she hadn't eaten since leaving the Governor's Office in D.C. early this morning, after being up all night before. Well maybe Chase had some staple food aboard and she could use this time to read back over the case files she had brought with her. There had to be something in the files that she was missing, some little but crucial piece of information that would be the key to solving the case.

Ashley ignored the twinge of nerves tightening between her shoulders - she refused to put the files down until she found something. Hours later, munching on crackers and soda; she felt nonetheless more anxious. What possible connection did the Aztec Chemical Company, The Colombian Drug Cartel and the disappearance of the governor's twenty three year old son have in common? The Aztec Chemical Company had recently relocated their corporate home office from D.C. to Florida; St. Andrews to be exact, a small seaside village about 40 miles down the coast from Bay City. Why move a billion dollar corporate office from a major metropolis like D.C. to a tourist trap like St. Andrews? It certainly wasn't for convenience or any other plausible or legal reason. So engrossed was she in the files, that Ashley barely registered the rainbow of pink and orange that was beginning to tinge the sky indicating that sunrise was imminent; nor did she hear the distant intermittent blaring horn of the approaching vessel.

"Florida Marine Patrol, is anyone aboard?" A distinct male voice blared.

Ashley jerked up from the bunk where she had dozed mere hours earlier; heart pounding as she reached for her gun. She emerged slowly from the downstairs cabin and up the steps to the dockside; peering around the doorframe. Ashley lowered her weapon as her eyes glanced quickly over the Marine Patrol boat. "I'm the only one on board." Ashley stated, stepping into the officers line of vision.

"Ma'am, are you okay? There was a terrible explosion down at the docks late last night and we were just canvassing the area to make sure everyone was accounted for and okay." The younger of the two marine patrol officers stared at her, awaiting a reply.

Ashley glanced from the older officer to the younger one and felt an odd since of familiarity about the older gentlemen. "Excuse me, but what is your name, sir?"

"Lt. Maddox, ma'am." He responded while gently touching the brim of his cowboy hat.

Ashley choked back a laugh; "Old Bureau Chief Maddox?" She inquired.

The older gentleman's eyes lit up with recognition; "Why Ash Cameron, it has been years since I last saw you." He sprinted from the marine patrol boat over to the deck of the cruiser to envelope her in a warm embrace. "How on earth have you been? I thought you had dropped off the face of the earth?"

She smiled at Maddox, "I've been okay, just staying really busy with my business in D.C., and I just came down for a visit to see some old friends. You don't look like you have been doing too bad either."

"Yeah, I guess I have put on a few pounds and lost a few hairs, the little lady takes real good care of me." Maddox replied while scratching his salt and pepper beard.

"Sounds like you found a great lady. Say can you guys do me a huge favor?"

"You name it Ash, and it is a done deal."

Ashley frowned. "Well, here is a card, I would like for you to contact this man and request that he meet, "a lady" don't use my name; at the Café Blue down at Lakewee Key at 10:00 a.m. this morning. Is the Café Blue still open?"

"Of course it is. That place is a landmark." Lt. Maddox replied.

"Please make contact with him in person. Don't use a land-line, cell or text message to relay the information. I know this may sound a little strange, but it is important that it be handled this way." Ashley explained.

Lt. Maddox puzzled smile broadened. "I will take care of it personally; I think your friend may have been the gentleman that requested we look for his boat and her occupant." Without waiting for a reply back, he disembarked from the cruiser and onto the marine patrol boat; waved a salute good-bye and soon the marine patrol boat became smaller and smaller until it diminished from view.

She had a few hours. After what she had read in

the files, more danger lie ahead; if she were right. It seemed that the Aztec Chemical Company had a very interesting dangerous, silent partner. If her basic instincts were still intact, she and Chase would have to move quickly before another murder occurred. She glanced at her wristwatch and headed out for Lakewee Key, there would be just enough time. About an hour later, a resonance ringing interrupted her train of thought. She glanced down at her cell phone clipped to her belt. It was a text message with a sequence of numbers followed by 911. Only she would know what it meant, Chase had received her message. They had worked together for so many years and had special codes so she knew he would have known it was her without being given a name. Soon, very soon she could explain everything she knew to him. He would certainly be glad to see his boat back safely at port. *Free Bird* had been Chase's pride and joy; the cruiser had been half blown up in a DEA Drug seizure years earlier and Chase had painstakingly brought her back to glowing restoration one piece at a time.

    The temperature was increasing rapidly. Ashley

decided as soon as she made port she had to shower and change. The humidity made your clothes cling to you like a second skin; she shielded her eyes over the top of her sunglasses as beads of perspiration slid down the sides of her face. She could barely catch the faint glimpse of land just ahead.

    After docking and anchoring the cruiser, she made her way down the corridor steps to the shower, so much for the nice long soaking bath she wanted to take. Handling the cruiser had drained her even further as it had been some time since she had handled a boat much less the monstrous *Free Bird*. The warm beads of water sprayed against her skin, easing some of the tension from her tired aching muscles. After donning a pair of white shorts and a black lightening streaked tank; Ashley surveyed her reflection in the mirror. Dark circles around her eyes, even make-up would not disguise. "Well, that is the best it gets, right?" Ashley questioned herself aloud while bending over to tie her tennis shoes. She locked and left the cabin cruiser, strolling across the boardwalk to the Café Blue on Bayfront Avenue.

Ashley glanced at her watch; she had fifteen minutes to spare. She found a corner booth and ordered a margarita on the rocks with extra salt. Looking around at the patrons and the wild array of ocean motif decor, she smiled. Some things never changed. Now that was a nice thought, for good things to never change. The Café Blue was a little place with a lot of atmosphere with its walls covered in dyed fishnets in an array of blues, yellows, greens and reds. Each net consisted of large conk shells, pieces of driftwood and numerous sprays of dried sea oats. It was one of the last of the original old businesses that scattered the coastline. Truly a landmark as Lt. Maddox had stated earlier. The waitress arrived with her drink and a sense of nostalgia settled over her. As she stared out the dusty pane windows at the waves crashing against the white sandy shore, she wondered if she would survive another case of this nature. There were numerous deeply painful wounds that had been inflicted, that had never healed, issues that Ash had refused to deal with, that maybe she had even ran from if the truth were known. She used to come here often, she used to believe in the justice system, she used to come here with Anthony, she used to be in love, she used to….. No, no, no; she told herself to stop. But the memories came flooding back like the rush of an incoming tide during a hurricane.

She had met Anthony Langston eight years ago while on assignment at Bay City. His long dark hair, dark eyes, tanned lean 6' 2" muscular body and a smile that could have melted the iceberg that crashed the titanic. He was on assignment with the Drug Enforcement Administration and they were partnered together to bring down the Colombian Drug Cartel running the Gulf Coast. It had taken them two years of deep undercover work before the indictments were handed down. The round-up that followed had gone haywire and she had almost been killed. They had ended up losing two DEA operative agents and an eight member SWAT team during that time. Donald, who had a wife and two children; and Alex, a confirmed bachelor with no apparent roots or known family; both worked with Ashley and Anthony.

All of their funerals had been within days of each other and she had been unable to attend due to being hospitalized in a coma. Healthcare staff had told her that Chase, Brenda, Gina Rae and Larry had remained vigil by her side the whole time she was hospitalized. Chase later told her about all the funeral arrangements, the flowers and who all had been present. Chase's wife Brenda, a pretty short petite redhead had stayed with her when Chase was at work during the day and Gina Rae, a petite strawberry blonde bombshell had stayed every night until her husband Larry had to leave for an overseas assignment. Brenda had been a wonderful friend and accepted Ashley as part of their family many years ago.

Brenda had been there for her when Anthony had just walked out of her life. This occurred only three months after Ashley had returned home from the hospital. She and Anthony had been arguing more often; he really wanted her to give up her job as a drug enforcement agent and she had refused. Anthony began to stay out drinking more and more and in the end he would stay gone for days at the time. They had argued bitterly and Ashley had left to meet the District Attorney to file additional warrants on some local drug smugglers. Ashley would never forget that day as long as she lived. The last thing she told Anthony was to kiss her ass, and she hoped he burnt in hell. She reached up and touched the scar beneath her ear and traced its path with her fingertips. The physical wounds had healed leaving behind many disfiguring scars; it was the internal wounds to the heart and soul that never healed. Shivering she recalled walking into the cottage after returning from the D.A.'s Office intending on telling Anthony she would do an early retirement and finding the letter by the bedside next to a single yellow rose; she still recalled every single word, like it was yesterday:

Dear Ash,
This is harder for me than you know.
Have a good life, you deserve it.
Anthony

The words had been ingrained in her heart and

soul for five long years now. Just eighteen words erased four years of her life with no real explanation; no I love you, nothing; although Anthony never really would say he loved you. Tony, as Ash referred to him was a perfectionist. Everything had to be just right and everything had a place; punctuality a must, if you were thirty seconds late, you were late, period. This was difficult for Ashley, her dad once told her the only event she would be on time for, would be her funeral because someone else would be doing that for her. Where Tony was concerned, if you didn't know why you did something, you simply did not do it - no excuses. They had been together every day and night for four years and yet at times she had felt like she barely knew him, like he was a stranger. Five years had come and gone without as much as a single word. He did not even know about his son, Anthony John, whom she called A. J. She had often felt guilty for not trying harder to find him, but, his few eighteen words had destroyed a big part of her and she didn't know where to look. That was her excuse anyway - for goodness sake she was a P.I., she could have found

Tony if she had really wanted to. She had heard the rumors that he had left town with an old girlfriend. A. J. was the only thing that kept her going in the beginning and he still was her reason for getting up every day. At least she still had a part of Tony with her every day. Tears started brimming in her blue eyes and she gently wiped them away. So much time had passed with no explanations and yet she could still see his face, longed for the feel of his touch, his kisses, and the aromatic scent of his cologne; like it was yesterday. Sometimes she felt like the deep recesses of her mind played tricks on her as she could actually smell his sexy masculine scent. Their relationship had been very volatile. Both of them were stubborn and headstrong - and their relationship had turned into a battle of wills at many times. They were both accustomed to having their own way and getting what they wanted. But she always told him how much she loved him, something she never heard in return. He used to say; "I show you, I shouldn't have to tell you, you should know and doesn't the fact that I am here count for anything?" Most of her friends didn't like Tony, they felt she deserved better, but she absolutely adored him even after the drunken binges of him staying gone for days; screw ups he had made, and she still loved him with all her heart. Gina Rae absolutely hated Tony. Her other friends just didn't understand how she could continue to love someone that put everything before their relationship. She had spent four years living on a roller coaster of heartstrings just by being with Tony and five years of pure hell afterwards, with him gone. That had to be a record. She had to admit to herself that it wasn't all heaven; there was a whole lot of pure hell. For every screw up he made she would kick him out of the house and throw his clothes out on the front lawn. Ashley had to admit that she was not without blame; for every indiscretion that Tony committed she would go out and buy something expensive like a thirty thousand dollar vehicle just to piss him off or get his attention. She had often felt that the only time Tony showed any emotion was when she did something totally absurd. If that didn't work, she buried herself in her job. But, she always accepted his pleas to return home. Even though their life had become like a roller coaster with extreme ups and downs, home just wasn't home without him, it was just a house.

It was ridiculous that coming to the Café Blue would incite all the pent up emotions she had smothered for years. They used to come here, pull up a bar stool, order margarita's, eat crab and close the place down. She glanced over at the jukebox sitting in the same corner it had years ago. Back then, Tony would pick her favorite selections of Eagles, Stones and Segar hits and sing karaoke and then go home and make passionate love until dawn. A few mornings she had gotten up and served him breakfast in bed, and he returned the favor many times as well. They would get up and make love in the shower before starting the day; she adored his long dark hair, his broad shoulders and rock hard muscled body.

If he didn't know where she was or what she was doing, he would call her constantly throughout the day on her cell phone or leave text messages. She missed Tony desperately, had loved him wholeheartedly, believed in him totally and had seen something in him that most people would never see; a lost soul searching for its destiny, lost somewhere on the horizon. Ashley had believed with every fiber of her being that she was his destiny. She knew she had been going through a grieving process, but damned it should be over by now. Ashley watched as a female patron left the jukebox after depositing money and making her selections. Her heart stopped beating as the beginning notes of a newer release, *Someone Like You* by a British Artist *Adele* began filling the air. She gently squeezed her eyes shut in an attempt to stop the tears from building in her eyes. The only other song she couldn't handle listening to was; *Colder Weather* by *Zac Brown*. Thinking of the words to that song, he was definitely a gypsy and would always leave you. She was singing the song silently in her head when the sound of keys clanking on the counter brought her out of her extremely painful memoirs.

"Hey, Ash, nice that you and *Free Bird* aren't crispy critters sharing the ocean floor with the sea crabs." Chase Brady's voice floated laughingly around her ears. "Would you care to provide any explanations to your old friend here? I mean within hours of your arrival, a whole port is blown to smithereens and a tag from a stolen vehicle that was leaving the area, just happens to be from D.C., no coincidence I would say. I don't know why I should be surprised considering your affinity with trouble".

"By all means, sit down." Ash answered while fidgeting with the margarita straw. Chase had always had a way of playing light of even the worst situations. Only those who knew him well would guess when he was really stressed.

Ash drew a deep breath, "Well to start with I received a panicked call from Uncle Morgan. You remember their son, my cousin Patrick. Patrick has coached my A. J.'s tee ball team for the past two years; he has always taken up a lot of time with A. J. teaching him to catch and how to throw the ball. My son is a typical four and a half year old and is very impressionable; Patrick is like a big brother to him, instead of a second cousin. Well anyway, Uncle Morgan called and Patrick has been missing for four weeks now, not a single call, nothing. Patrick had just started a part time job with the Aztec Chemical Company as a Securities Marketing Specialist Data Programmer about three months ago. Uncle Morgan said that Patrick's behavior had changed drastically a few weeks before he went missing; staying out all hours, not eating, and very evasive when asked about his new job. He begged me to help him and I agreed to do a background investigation into Aztec Chemical Company. For starters, they have offices scattered along the coasts; California, Mexico, New Orleans, Mobile, Miami, Cayman Islands, Colombia South America and about a month ago they relocated a portion of their Corporate Office in D.C. to none other than St. Andrews, Florida."

"Do you mean less than an hour down the coast from here?" Chase choked on his drink.

Ashley sighed. "Yes, that would be the one. Anyway, through searching the business license and various corporate activities there appears to be a silent partner - Adrianno Martinelli. Yes, I can tell by the look on your face. The one and only - master mind for the

Colombian Drug Cartel, remember we indicted his son years ago but, were unable to touch him. More interesting, is the fact that Martinelli's Cartel is controlled by the local Dixie Mafia. The Dixie Mafia has always concentrated their money laundering activities in the gulf coast along the lines of bars, strip clubs, restaurants and car dealerships; so a Chemical Company is a little odd. It doesn't take a lot to figure out why all the offices are strategically located at major port cities. But the one exception is St. Andrews; it is a tourist trap and has a small out of the way secluded beach area away from the downtown district. It just makes no sense, the airport is very small. But past experience has proven that they don't necessarily need an airport, they can make a landing strip out of any fairly straight and halfway secluded stretch of land and a half dozen flares. I have chased down every friend that Patrick had in D.C. and shortly after starting to work for Aztec Chemical, he cut off all his friends. A. J. had tried to call him several times and he did not even return his calls. It is like Patrick has just vanished in thin air. Aunt Lynn and Uncle Morgan are both frantic with worry. He is after all their only child. Lynn asked me to leave A. J. with them while I was gone. So he is keeping them very occupied I am sure."

Ashley took a sip of her drink nervously twitching the straw around the edges. "An inside source at the Chemical Company revealed to me that several men were fired about four weeks ago due to a capsized ship carrying unknown classified cargo. I hit the street and found a confidential informant that revealed that the cargo was none other than a cool six million in cocaine. But, other than some extremely 'high" marine animals for a short period of time, there is no proof. The time frame matches up with when Patrick vanished. My first thought was that for some unknown reason Patrick was aboard that ship. I contacted the Marine Patrol and the incident report made available to me stated that all parties aboard the ship survived. The manifest containing passengers is like a who's who list for the Drug Cartel and Dixie Mafia. I have researched additionally through Interpol (international police) and there have been several ongoing investigations into the Aztec Chemical Company over the past four years however, the containers they ship the chemicals in are sealed airtight and drug dogs at the ports have been unsuccessful in hitting on the scent."

Ashley inhaled deeply then continued, "Upon further investigation, I discovered that due to the nature of some of the chemicals and the government contracts awarded to Aztec; their containers have a metal lining which is made of the same material as military aircraft for shielding them from radar; Indium oxide and tin oxide combined to form indium tin oxide, a transparent optical coating that blocks infrared rays. The thin metal lining of these containers are coated with this oxide. So they can't be scanned for content and they can't be sniffed out by drug dogs. Which means you would have to rely on an inside undercover agent and there have been two in the last four years that died suspiciously in the line of duty prior to them testifying before the grand jury, so no indictments were handed down. One died while attempting to apprehend a burglar in an apartment complex when the burglar took his .357 service revolver and shot him in the head and the other was murdered after he stopped the robber of a liquor store; again with his on service revolver a .357 - shot in the head. Neither murder was ever considered a Cartel or Mafia hit even though they occurred within a year of each other in adjacent counties."

Chase grunted. "There was probably another one; do you remember David Sims that worked for DEA about 8 years ago?"

Ashley shook her head in acknowledgment.

"Well, he was working an undercover operation involving a chemical company who sold out to another large conglomerate several years ago. He was very deep under and the central office only had a few notes and the several case files saved on his computer were converted to disk but they were in code. No one has been able to decipher them to my knowledge. Anyway he and his wife and three year old daughter died in a house fire. The Fire Marshall ruled it accidental as faulty wiring, but the house was site built just three years earlier, it is possible but I doubted the marshal's decision. I always felt that it was a direct hit and not an accident. We need to pull those files also and see who bought that chemical company. I would lay you money that its new owner is or is connected to Adrianno Martinelli."

"I wonder whose pocket the Fire Marshall was in; the Cartel or the Mafia?" Ashley asked, while rubbing her temples.

"Maybe, both!" "DEA does have a new kid that is a whiz at deciphering code and encrypted messages. He has only been with us about three months, but is a computer genius. I will pull those files, notes and disk from his hard drive and get them on his desk immediately."

It was Ashley's turn to choke on her drink, "That would mean two Agents and a family of three murdered already!" Ashley grimaced.

"Ash, who all knows that you are here?" Chase interrupted.

Ashley frowned, "Only my Office Manager Gina Rae, her husband Larry which is my Chief Investigator, Uncle Morgan and Aunt Lynn, Why?"

Chase cleared his throat deeply. "Ash you have

stumbled onto something here and I am not sure just how deep or how far up the political food chain it goes. But, you can rest assured that the explosion at the docks was intended to stop you before you could find the answers. You need to call the Governor and make sure that they take extra precautions with A. J. and themselves until we can get to the bottom of this. I don't need to remind you that years ago before your Uncle took the D.C. job; he was the Governor in Alabama. That was when we had all the problems in Phoenix City when it was controlled by the Dixie Mafia! I will send Vince up to D.C. as a personal body guard for A. J. immediately. Trent, a buddy of mine has a cottage kind of off the beaten path between here and Bay City. It sits on two acres and is chain link fenced all around the property with an excellent security system. It is prime ocean front property that was left to him by his grandparents and only three people know about its' location. He is a real estate mortgage broker and is out of the country for awhile. You should be safe there and ----"

"We are just letting our imaginations and

adrenalin run away with us! Stop Chase, Is all this really necessary?" Ashley demanded.

Now, Chase rubbed his forehead, "Yes it is definitely necessary. If Martinelli and his men are behind Patrick's disappearance, you know what they are capable of doing. You do remember you almost got yourself killed nearly six years ago, the last time we tangled with the Martinelli Cartel. Not to mention the two contract hits on your life right before that by the Mafia. We will go to the boat and secure all your belongings and I will take you up there myself. I will get DEA to issue you a new laptop computer, and cell phone which is a blackberry; the two will be linked for email purposes. You don't need to use the ones that you brought with you anymore, there is a possibility they could be traced. The Director for DEA is still Madison and he advised me earlier that he will swear you in and issue you a badge on a temporary basis while you are here working." Ashley looked so far away that Chase was unsure if she was even still listening to him. Do you understand me?"

"Yes, Chase" sighing dejectedly, Ashley knew that

Chase was right.

She was just having a hard time accepting the fact that she was once again working for DEA, and once again back in the Emerald Coast of Florida. Maybe it was called the Emerald Coast for the "green" or dirty blood money of its organized crime leaders. Chase motioned for the waitress and scribbled his name on the slip of paper for the tab for their drinks. He and Ashley exited the back door of the Café Blue. The back door opened up to an alley of white sand. The mid-day sun reflected off the bleached white granules as bright as lighting streaks. As they walked around the side of the Cafe', Ashley squinted her eyes and fished frantically in her purse for her oversized sunglasses to dull the contrast from the cool café lights to the mid-day bright reflections from the sun. She was getting a migraine. In less than twenty four hours her mind and body had been tormented from lack of sleep, lack of food, nearly being killed and the floodgates opening on painful memories she had spent five years running away from. Fate had to have something in store for her; she just wasn't sure she wanted to find out what, right now. But find out is exactly what she would have to do. Her favorite quote came to mind, *The past is lost in a sea of darkness forever and the future is but a faint glimpse on the horizon.* Well, the painful memories from the past would just have to stay that for now - in the past……

"Ash, Ash, ASHLEY ! , Are you going to get in the car, or just stand outside daydreaming while the rest of our daylight fades away?" Chase shouted.

"I'm getting in smart ass." Ashley replied sarcastically while opening the passenger side door and crawling in the car. She had been so absorbed in her own thoughts that she had not realized that Chase had opened the passenger door and was already in the driver's seat with the engine running and ready to drive off. The cool rich leather seats of the Jaguar felt so comfortable after standing in the hot sun only momentarily. She had forgotten how hot and humid the summers were in Florida. She had forgotten a lot of things associated with Florida, but then again, some things were better off forgotten.

Ashley's thoughts wondered back to Tony as they often did. If there was a man on earth who could touch and kiss better than Tony, God had blessed the woman who had caught him. Tony had the most beautiful hands and sensuous mouth, and he knew how to use them. She still wanted those hands and that mouth on her, too. It had nearly killed her for almost five years now, not knowing where he was or if he was dead or alive. She had too much pride to ever search for him though, after so long. And even if she did; what good would it do? Tony's little eighteen words had made it perfectly clear that he was through with her. Besides he had made no effort to track her down and find her, and she knew with his past work experience that he could have easily located her if he had so desired, just as easily as she could have located him, her inner voice reminded her.

She often had regrets for A. J. to grow up never knowing his father. And, A.J. was getting old enough to start asking more questions than the few she had fielded in the past. A.J. was the mirror image of his father, dark hair, dark eyes, and same high cheekbones.

Ashley gazed out the windows at the passing scenery. Bleached white sand dunes held up by large bunches of sea oats dotted the coastline to prevent the ebb and flow of the ocean tide from swallowing up the land. The crashing waves against the shore looked peaceful as they flipped the little shells and sand dollars up onto the beach for the children to collect. An occasional seagull dipped down scavenging for crumbs left behind by beachcombers, as the bright colored sails of the boats glistened in the distance. It was breathtaking how the ocean met the horizon; they just seemed to melt into each other like lovers in the night. She had forgotten how much she had loved living on the beach and all its beauty.

"How are Gina Rae and Larry?" Chase asked, sensing Ashley's tension and trying to engage her in a pleasant conversation.

"They are doing good. Gina Rae has the business knowledge to keep all the financial aspects of my business afloat and Larry can solve any crime." Ashley replied, smiling halfheartedly.

"I still remember the time I stopped you and Gina Rae on the cut-off road from the beach. I think you guys had left a party somewhere when I drove up behind you driving about forty, slowing down, opening both doors, two heads sticking out the doors, looking around, then closing them and driving a few more miles before repeating the same scenario." Chase laughed loudly.

"We were drunk, I was driving and opened my door to find the center line and Gina Rae opened her door on the passenger side to find the outside line in the highway. We were trying to stay between the lines. That is when we were young and stupid, now we just drink at home by a fire and don't drive." Ashley shook her head laughing with a huge smile on her face.

"I know you stopped in the middle of the road when I threw the blue lights on your car. You guys were both trashed, I had to call Larry and Tony to come and drive you both home." Chase smirked.

Ashley laughed. "Larry drove my car and Tony followed us to pick Larry up. They took us back to my house on the beach and told us not to leave again. They were working some stake-out that night. The only problem with that plan was that I had just moved to another house, and neither Gina nor I told them. We waited until they left and got back in the car and drove around with rock-n-roll music blaring through the speakers until almost daylight."

"I know, they relieved me on that stake-out that night and the next day when they were talking about taking you both home to get your drunken butts off the road; I died laughing because I knew you had moved. I always liked Gina Rae and Larry and was really surprised when they divorced, even more surprised when they remarried ten years later!" Chase looked at Ashley with a puzzled expression.

"That is a whole different story. Larry was always tall, muscular and handsome and had women dropping like flies at this feet. You know the cop groupie types. He fell to that temptation and Gina Rae stomped the little bitches ass and almost kicked his ass too, one of county deputies called me to come and get her that night. He had her in the back of the patrol car and she almost kicked out the windows. They were divorced soon after that happened. You were working deep undercover in South America at that time." Ashley shook her head.

"Well how the hell did they end up back together after so long?" Chase asked bemused.

"Let's just say, a small fire and a lot of *patron*...."

"Oh, no. You can't drink tequila!" he looked over at her.

"I can hold my own. And, to answer your question; Gina Rae never got over Larry, she never stopped loving him. She married someone else but it didn't last very long. It was New Year's Eve and she and I were drinking around a fire pit in my back yard. Gina Rae said she wondered what ever happened to Larry and would love to talk to him again. She said she didn't know where he was anymore. I made some phone calls and within a couple of hours I had located him. I dialed his number and handed her the phone to listen to the voicemail and asked her if she recognized that voice. She almost died. They met shortly afterwards and within six months, I married them for the second time." Ashley said with a smile that came straight from her heart.

"Gina Rae is so petite, but dynamite does come in small packages. She was a looker with that long strawberry blonde hair and curves that never ended. I was surprised he strayed." he said.

"Me too, but they were both young and worked all the time back then. They are inseparable now."

"Isn't she is the daughter of that millionaire logging and trucking tycoon, O'Marley?" Chase asked.

"Yes, but they haven't been close for years. Gina Rae never approved of his business ethics, or lack of them!" Ashley frowned.

They had driven miles down the abandoned seacoast with the road having veered so far from the coast that the seashore was barely still visible. Chase braked hard after almost passing the sandy dirt trail that curved back toward the shore.

"You still can't drive worth a damn." Ashley muttered as she almost smacked the windshield with her head.

"Yeah, well I am not the one that wrecked four

federal vehicles in 12 years, now am I smart mouth?" Chase laughingly replied.

"No, your record was two vehicles, three boats, a plane and a chopper. The only difference is you prefer water and air. And might I remind you there are fewer boats in the water and choppers in the air than there are vehicles on the road, so you are more accident prone than I am." Ashley smugly retorted.

Chase laughed deeply. "You know you may have a point there, but we are at the cottage so you can stop worrying."

"Cottage!" Ashley exclaimed. "This place is huge."

Chase keyed numbers into the keypad and the electronic gates opened up revealing a beautiful two story cottage type stucco home painted in a pale mint green with pink flamingo sculptures gracing the wrap around deck. Massive palm trees provided shading all across the front deck and for the L-shaped pool on the north side of the home.

"This is really a piece of paradise, Chase." Ashley

said as she wandered around the L-shaped living/dining room of the cottage home. There were ceiling to floor windows that held a spectacular view of the ocean just down below, the entrance foyer was a large octagon shape of real hardwood flooring.

Ashley glanced around at the rather sparsely furnished home, with its peach seashell printed carpet and pale lime walls. She especially liked the king size white wicker sofa and rocker with their oversized ocean print cushions. Above the white stone fireplace she spotted two oil paintings that looked a little out of place with the other furnishings. They were excellent reproductions of *Starry Starry Night* and *Irises* by artist *Vincent van Gogh*.

"It is pretty cool. The bedrooms are upstairs." Chase replied from the kitchen area. "I like the lack of frills and clutter you see in a lot of the beach homes." Chase busied himself with checking all the locks on the doors and windows.

"You know *Vincent van Gogh* is my favorite artist, the guy really has good taste." Ashley stated admiring the pieces of art.

"Good taste? Displaying art from a guy that cut his ear off and sent it to his lady!" Chase laughed.

"You are an ass." Ashley called back to Chase as she climbed the stairs to the master bedroom and placed her suitcases at the foot of the enormous king size bed, shrouded in a comforter of none other than *Irises* also by artist *Van Gogh*. The drapes and wallpaper in the adjoining bathroom suite were also of the same print. The massive marble Jacuzzi tub had to be her greatest discovery yet. It looked so inviting. Ashley was interrupted from her relaxing thoughts by the musical tempo of *As Time Goes By* it was Chase's cell phone ringing. He had downloaded that stupid ring tone. As she descended the stairs she heard Chase's voice reassuring someone that she was okay. It had to be Brenda; there wasn't anyone else that knew she was here that would be worried.

"Yes, Brenda she is fine. I should be home in about forty five minutes and I will fill you in then. Yes, I have her in a safe place and, yes she will eat dinner with us tomorrow night. I think she is just exhausted right now, I will bring you out to see her tomorrow and you can spend the day catching up on all the news. But we have a lot of work to complete in a short period of time. Love ya, and see you shortly."

Ashley's eyes misted over. "I would love to see Brenda, she is like a sister to me and I have missed her terribly."

Chase snorted. "You don't have to live with her daily. She can be a real bitch, but I love her anyway. I better get going, everything here is secure. Feel free to use the red jeep in the garage, the keys are hanging on the wall in the kitchen, Trent won't mind. But, I wouldn't recommend you start running all over town immediately. I checked the freezer and there is plenty of food, Trent usually keeps the place well stocked. You would think he expected a world famine from the looks of his food stockpile. He really went overboard years ago with the Y2K thing. He could have fed the whole State of Florida for a month, a little over a decade and he still hasn't depleted all that food. I will bring the files I told you about over here tomorrow once I have downloaded them for the analyst to review and the other stuff from the office. You really need to stay put until we can get a handle on what is really going on with Martinelli and his goons."

Ashley hugged Chase bye. "I don't plan on going anywhere tonight, I am totally wiped out and I am really getting a migraine. I imagine the time difference, flying, almost getting blown up, sailing, too much sun, too much stress, too little sleep, too many memories……. you name it. Thanks again for everything and tell Brenda I can't wait to see her tomorrow. I will talk to you when I get up in the morning."

Chase scribbled numbers on a piece of notepad and handed it to her. "Put this in a safe place, it is the security combination for the doors and the outer gates, don't forget to double bolt the doors and --"

Ashley put up her hand. "Yes I know, double bolt the doors, turn the alarm system on, don't use any of my phones, don't answer the door for anyone I don't know… blah, blah, blah. I will use the landline here to call A. J. and check in with my office later. Just let me know how to reimburse your friend Trent." She stuck her tongue out at Chase as she walked him to the door, double bolted the locks and set the alarm system as he had shown her before climbing the stairs to start the dreamy Jacuzzi bath running.

She only hoped she didn't fall asleep and drown she mused as she turned the brass faucets to start the warm water running before flipping the switch for the pulsing water jets. She turned on the sound system and a *Beethoven* melody, *Moonlight Sonata* began softly filling the room. Ashley found a bottle of aspirin and some luxurious gardenia scented bath salts in the linen closet and generously sprinkled them in the marble bath before disrobing and sliding into its heavenly scented waters. She choked down three aspirin hoping they would work and that she would not need her migraine medicine because it made her really groggy and fuzzy headed. She just wanted to relax and stop her tortuous thoughts from consuming her for a little while before climbing into bed, now that shouldn't be too much to ask. There would be time for unpleasant thoughts tomorrow. Yes indeed, she would pretend to be Scarlet from, *Gone with the Wind*, *"I'll think about it tomorrow.... Tomorrow is another day."*

CHAPTER THREE

Ashley woke up abruptly at 7:30 am. There was a repeated loud banging on the front door, and obnoxious sounding chimes ringing throughout the house. Grouchily she crawled out of bed, screaming towards the downstairs front door, "I'll be down in a minute." After tripping on the ruffle of the bed comforter and nearly knocking herself out on the bedpost, she snatched on a pair of "Scooby" boxers and an oversized t-shirt and ran downstairs.

"What do you want?" She snapped, yanking the front door open.

"Well, Miss Grouchy; if that isn't a fine welcome; I don't know what is?" Brenda Brady laughingly teased with her elegant southern drawl overly exaggerated.

Ashley reached out and hugged Brenda while

glaring over her shoulder at Chase. "Do you know what time it is?"

"Way past time to be up enjoying the day", Chase growled as he sat doughnuts and milk on the counter. "And, I am sure you knew who was at the door before you just yanked it open?"

Ashley ignored him, surveying her best friend from head to toe. Brenda looked gorgeous, dressed in a silky black halter top with a shiny short white skirt. She was an expert at accessorizing with big black/white bangles of woven seashells; and white sand dollar earrings to match. So petite with her springy red hair peeking out from beneath the oversized white sunhat she wore. She always looked like she had stepped directly off the pages of Vogue or Cosmopolitan magazines. "Brenda, you look fabulous. I have missed you so much."

"Too bad the looks don't match the personality!" Chase smirked.

"You should know!" Brenda chirped, as she slapped him in the head with her sunhat.

"Well I hate to bust up the family reunion but on

a more serious note, I have to get into the office and pick up the computer and cell phone that I promised to bring out to you, Ash. The cell phones that DEA uses now are "B*lack*B*erry*" with direct connect, text, internet and camera/video, you name it, the best in technology. I will program all the numbers you will need and have our IT tech link the e-mail to DEA's databases. I am also going to pick up the old case files for us to review; some of the newer files will be on thumb drives so you can just pop them into your laptop and download. They may give us some additional leads. Martinelli Cartel men were the ones driving the stolen black Lincoln from D.C. that was entering the docks after I dropped you off; prior to the explosion. All three men had rap sheets that would wallpaper this room and were covered in tattoos indicative of the "Black Devils Drug Gang." Explosive device mechanisms were found in the stolen car when the police stopped them. The crime lab identified the explosives at the scene and matched up the types to what was found in their car so we have enough probable cause to charge them and hold them. We tried every legal and not so legal means of persuasion to get the bastards to talk, but they wouldn't give up a thing. We interrogated them individually for two hours each and nothing. I feel certain that they followed you from D.C. since the car was stolen from the airport there. They had to have known your flight plan and left D.C. long before you boarded the plane. I am sure they also anticipated a long layover in Atlanta for them to have made it to the Airport by the time your flight landed; and followed us to the docks at Bay City. I have already called Vince in D.C. and the Governor's phone was tapped, hence the information they needed to follow you, which also meant that your instincts were correct in linking Martinelli to Patrick's disappearance. I should be back by lunch and I will take you ladies out to the *Lobster Lodge* to eat. Try not to destroy anything or anyone until then!" Chase gave the girls a mock salute and left them to their own devices for the morning.

Just as Chase drove away the phone at the cottage rang. Assuming it was Chase already calling them; Ashley answered in a sweet exaggerated southern voice, "darlin' you miss us already?"

"Well you know I miss my number one niece, but I somehow don't think I am the caller of your expectations." laughed Ashley's Uncle Morgan, trying to hide the strain in his voice.

"Uncle Morgan, I am so sorry." Ashley detected the tremor in his laugh but chose not to elaborate on the fact. "You have your number one niece, because I am the only niece you have. You remember my friend Chase with DEA, I thought you were him as he just left Brenda here with me. He went into the office to bring back equipment and files we need to follow up on leads with the case. Have you heard anything from Patrick yet?"

"That is why I am calling, I'm sure Chase told you about the phone tap on my lines. They have cleared everything and secured all my lines. The D.C. Police pulled Patrick's Camaro out of the river about four o'clock this morning. They are sending a dive team down now to see if they can recover the body. It doesn't look like an accident according to the State Police Report, they pulled in the Accident Reconstructive Team and there were absolutely no skid marks, like he just accelerated and drove straight off into the river. There is no curve in the road or anything at the point the car went off the road. From the looks of everything they believe the car had been in the river three to four weeks. Ash, you know Patrick would never have just driven off into the river." Uncle Morgan voice cracked with emotion on that last bit of information.

"I am so sorry and I know you are right, I don't believe that Patrick would do something like that either. Please keep me informed and can you have the State Police fax copies of everything they have to the DEA Office down here to the attention of Agent Chase Brady. Maybe there is something in them that will help us with the investigation down here. Is A. J. okay there with you and Aunt Lynn right now? I know she has to be devastated and I can send for him if you need me to."

"Oh, no." Uncle Morgan quickly recovered his composure. A. J. is really keeping Lynn's spirits up right now. They went down to the stables this morning to go horseback riding. He was so excited when you called him last night and such a little man. When he hung up he patted Lynn on the back and told her "don't worry, momma will bring Uncle Pat home safe."

"Well, if you are sure he is no problem I will let him stay."

"Please do, and thank Chase for me. Vince the bodyguard he sent up here arrived at four-thirty am this morning and he is monitoring their every move. I will be in touch later today."

Ashley stood for a few minutes listening to the rapid dial tone indicating the caller had long terminated the call. She hoped that Uncle Morgan was right. Yes, she knew that he was right; Patrick would never commit suicide no matter what was going on in his life. He simply did not believe that was permissible or forgivable in Gods eyes.

"Honey, what's going on?" Brenda gently took the phone from Ashley's unresisting hand and placed it back in its charger.

Ashley misty eyed, relayed her Uncles conversation to Brenda. "I just know that Patrick is okay.

I offered to send for A. J. but they want him to stay there. Vince is there as their bodyguard."

"Chase told me he had sent Vince, he is really good and he won't let anything happen to them. If you want A. J. here, you know he can stay with me, I would love having him here."

"Brenda, I worry so much about A. J. He is all I have. You know he looks just like his daddy and he has gotten old enough to start asking questions about his father. I don't know what to tell him because I don't know where Tony is or what has happened to him. There have been so many times over the past five years that I have wanted to find him and tell him about A. J. but then another part of me doesn't want to. If he had cared about me, he just would never have been able to leave like he did. I tried once to find him, but not hard enough."

"You know I thought I saw him in town a couple of years ago, riding a Harley motorcycle with a group of bikers. I could have sworn that it was him but Chase insisted that I must have been mistaken that Tony left the bureau when he left you and nobody has seen or heard anything from him since." Brenda smiled reassuringly at Ashley.

"I don't know what I would do if I saw him again; kiss him, slap him or shoot him. You know Brenda, I still love Tony but, a part of me hates him at the same time. He wasn't there for me the last year and a half we were together when I really needed him the most."

"Ashley, you never told him you had cancer. It took a while for me to get it out of you, but; I knew something was wrong. You kept losing weight, getting paler and paler and disappearing for days with no explanation. You would surface after saying you were working and be in the bed for days. You stopped going anywhere with Tony. I mean I know you guys worked things out and everything seemed better the last year you were together, you were better and seemed like the old couple again."

Ashley took a deep breath. "He had started drinking so much, staying gone for days, and sleeping on the couch. I just couldn't tell him and see the pity in his eyes, or wonder if he were staying with me because I was sick and not out of love. Besides near the end when I was actually well, I always wondered if he were seeing someone else. I had some friends tell me they saw him at the bar with a woman a couple of times. I still remember it like yesterday, in the beginning of my treatments, I had been through a week of chemo and radiation and was so sick and he was out drinking with one of his old flames. That wasn't the first time either, there were many nights I was home alone after days of treatments when I was throwing my guts up, couldn't eat, couldn't sleep and he was always in a bar somewhere drinking with his buddies.

"I often regretted not telling Tony once I knew you were sick. I remember taking you and picking you up from treatments and begging you to tell him. Later, do you think things would have been different if he had known you were pregnant?"

Ashley almost snorted with disgust. "Well, damn I didn't know until two months after he left, remember, and besides I wanted him to love me for me not just because he felt obligated to do so. I was so happy the year before when I received the diagnosis that I was cancer free but that paled in comparison to knowing I was having Tony's child. At that point I was so worried that something would be wrong with my unborn child because of all the treatments I had been through twelve months earlier."

"I know, I know. But, afterwards did you ever try to find him?" Brenda picked up the milk and doughnuts and ushered Ashley into the kitchen, rummaging through cabinets until she located plates and glasses.

"I did try a couple of times the first few months with no luck, but like I said earlier; not really hard. I have thought about trying again to get in touch with him, but after over five years it seems pointless now, why do you ask?" Ashley took the plate of doughnuts that Brenda offered.

"Maybe he has grown up finally, you know even the really bad boys do grow up eventually and become real men."

"Well, enough about Tony for now, he is probably still with one of his bleached blonde, tattooed bimbos. I need to concentrate on finding out what has happened to Patrick. You know, I think I want to check out the job availability at the new corporate offices for Aztec Chemical Company near here. Just to get a feel for things and snoop around a little….."

"Ashley Cameron, Chase will kill you." Brenda interrupted with a screech. "You know he told you to sit tight and wait until he gets back with all the files and equipment."

"And I will, but after lunch I will go down to the Chemical Plant. You are not going to tell Chase, what he doesn't know want hurt him now will it?" Ashley smiled mischievously.

Ashley and Brenda continued chatting catching up on lost time and before they knew it Chase was at the front door. Chase delivered all the computer equipment and phones as promised. The trio headed toward the *Lobster Lodge* for lunch. Chase gave Ashley a strange look when she persisted in driving the jeep and following them to the restaurant rather than them all riding together.

"Brenda, what is Ashley up to? Why did she

insist on driving the jeep? Why didn't she want to ride with us?"

"I don't know, I don't know and I don't know. Why must you interrogate me with numerous questions at a time? You don't give me a chance to answer the first one before you pop off two or three more. You know I hate it when you do that, yet you persist in doing so every time you ask a question; no, not just a question but two or three. I am your wife not some suspect you are interrogating." Brenda snapped, silently hoping that her short tirade would throw Chase off track and he would not ask her anymore questions as she had reluctantly promised Ashley that she would not say anything about her afternoon plans.

"Okay, my lovely wife, I am sorry." Sorry I asked you too many questions at once, it is a habit." Chase reached over and patted her on the leg. They argued constantly but he worshiped the ground Brenda walked on and could not imagine his life without her. That did not mean however that he did not realize how close she and Ashley had always been and Brenda would cover for

Ashley in a minute and vice-versa. He would just let it slide for the time being and let her think her little tirade had proven distracting.

The *Lobster Lodge* was packed for its usual lunchtime crowd. The tantalizing smell of fresh steamed lobster filled its clapboard interior. The trio was seated at a corner booth in the back of the restaurant as Brenda laughed waiting for Chase and Ashley to finish arguing over seating as neither would sit with their back to the entrance. Wooden bench type tables were covered with red and white checkered cloths, and old vintage bottles of wine turned into flower vases filled with an array of spring dried flowers.

"Chase, my man, what's up?" A tall good-looking dark haired, gray-eyed man wearing a black Stetson hat, tight faded jeans and a black polo shirt with an embroidered star had approached their table.

"Not much sheriff, how's it going?" Chase responded by shaking his hand.

"Just fighting crime, you know how that goes." The sheriff smiled admiringly at Ashley.

"Sheriff Don Bates, this is Ashley Cameron. She is an old friend of ours, and worked for twelve years with the DEA some time back." Chase made the introductions.

"Pleasure to meet you Sheriff Bates." Ashley shook his preferred hand.

"Ma'am, the pleasure is all mine, and call me Don." Sheriff Bates informed her while touching the brim of his hat. I was elected sheriff here four years ago, just ran again so I will be starting my second term soon. Let me know if I can be of any assistance during your visit here."

Ashley was glad that she was spared a response to his suggestive offer of assistance, as a patron of the restaurant engaged Sheriff Bates into a serious seemingly political conversation.

"What are you two smirking at?" Ashley snapped at Chase and Brenda once Sheriff Bates was out of hearing range.

Brenda smiled. "He was just letting you know he was eligible."

"He is a real catch, he likes jumping out of helicopters over the ocean while holding onto his cowboy hat!" Chase tried to sound sincere but failed miserably.

"Eligible for what, would be a better question. Oh, don't get me wrong he is one fine looking man but he knows it, and another egotistical asshole is not what I need in my life. Been there and done that one already. My experience with drop dead gorgeous men has been; they are either a plant trying to find information, a mean drunk, corrupt or just a pure ass!" Ashley wasn't sure why they were both staring at her but it was time to order lunch. She was starving. "I will have the steamed lobster, spinach salad with balsamic and unsweetened tea with lemon" Ashley told the waitress who was waiting to take her order as she had already taken Chase and Brenda's.

Chase decided it was time to tread the waters to find out what Ashley was up to. "So what do you ladies have planned for this afternoon?"

Ashley narrowed her eyes at Brenda's choking sounds. "Just thought I would go into town and pick up some essentials that I left behind in D.C., Brenda has other things she has to do. Chase, I forgot to tell you, I heard from Uncle Morgan this morning after you left…"

Brenda interrupted, "If you both will excuse me I need to freshen up, Ashley go ahead and fill Chase in on the events of the morning." Brenda was bubbling inside with laughter as she exited the table because it was so evident that Ashley had abruptly changed the subject, not that the discussion wasn't important - she was sure that was why Ashley had chosen this particular moment to relay this information - a legitimate distraction!

Several minutes later Brenda returned to the table to find Chase and Brenda engrossed in conversation.

"I will check the fax at my office for the D.C. Police Reports on the accident and drop those off to you tonight. Craig has a baseball game that starts at 8 o'clock tonight so it will be after the game is over." Chase ordered a round of refills for their drinks.

"Craig is sixteen now isn't he?" Ashley asked.

"Yes, and still a typical spoiled only child. It is not his fault though; Chase and I made him that way." Brenda quickly defended her son. "He has the highest

RBI in the district and has made All-Stars for the last four years. I am so proud of him. But, he has a new girlfriend that I don't particularly like...."

"She could be Princess Diana or Mother Teresa reincarnated and you still wouldn't like her or any other girl he picks out." Chase interrupted. "None of them will ever be good enough for our little boy."

Ashley laughed as Brenda and Chase started arguing again. Soon they had all finished their lunch and it was time to go.

"I will see you both tonight, tell Craig I hope they win, and I will try to catch one of his games before I go back to D.C." Ashley headed out to the parking lot to the jeep. She waited until Brenda and Chase climbed in the Jaguar and waved goodbye. Ashley pretended to be touching up her makeup in the rear view mirror as she watched until they were out of site before she pulled onto the highway headed out of town -- toward the Industrial Park Exit, Aztec Chemical Company to be more exact.

"Industrial Park Exit, twelve miles." Ashley read the sign aloud about an hour later. She had exited the

Interstate twice in order to lose what she assumed was a "FED" vehicle - someone that Chase had obviously put on her tail to follow her. Ashley hoped it was someone Chase had sent to tail her, either way she wasn't having it. The first guy she lost pretty quickly but the other one required her to ride around a good five minutes and slip into an alley between two dilapidated old buildings and waiting about five minutes before getting back on the Interstate. She would soon see just what was going on at this Chemical Plant. Ashley pulled the Jeep into the entrance marked "personnel" and stopped to check in at the security gate. Luckily they were accepting applications today so the security guard gave her a visitor pass, directions and motioned for her to continue on to the parking lot. Twelve feet high chain link fencing with razor wire surrounded the entire plant with security guards at four separate check points. Above each entrance there were cameras monitoring all employees and visitors that entered and exited the plant. Ashley parked the Jeep and headed into the plant entrance marked personnel. Just as she was entering the plant her cell phone started ringing. It had to be Chase because no one else would have the new number this quickly. She looked down at the phone and recognized Chase's private line at DEA. Ashley looked at the entrance door and back down at the ringing phone and hesitated only briefly before simply shutting the phone off, she would deal with Chase later.

Ashley proceeded down a long corridor that opened up into a foyer containing a glass cubicle with a smiling blonde haired receptionist inside. She waited in line behind several other people obviously applying for jobs.

"Can I help you?" The receptionist inquired through the small square opening in the cubicle.

"Yes, I would like to see what jobs you have available." Ashley inquired.

"There is a list on the bulletin board of posted vacancies along with clipboards and applications. Feel free to fill out as many applications as you would like, making sure you include the job number for the position for which you are interested. You will need to fill out an application for each position and return them to me before you leave. You may also visit our website and complete the applications online. There are brochures which contain our plant history and maps to our various locations on the table." The receptionist turned away before Ashley could thank her for the information.

Ashley scanned the job openings pretending to write information down in the portfolio she had brought with her. She picked up several of the brochures and maps the receptionist had indicated, noting in particular that their main warehouse was located behind the brick wall separating the plant from and adjacent to the major port in the city. That would be a good place to start surveillance. Ashley noticed that all employees had the photo identification tags that contained magnetic stripping for access throughout secure areas in the plant. The employees simply swiped the cards across a sensor which would in turn electronically open doors to allow them to gain entrance to specified areas of the plant. Probably different staff had certain security levels pre-approved for admittance. She made herself a note to check with Uncle Morgan about Patrick's I.D. Since Patrick was a Securities Marketing Specialist Data Programmer he would have had a high level security clearance which should still be active unless Aztec Chemical had de-activated his clearance; and if that were the case she would need to know when it was deactivated. This could prove the Companies involvement in Patrick's disappearance. If by chance her Uncle or Aunt could locate the I.D. in Patrick's belongings - it would prove useful. In the past, Ashley had hacked several computer systems and acquired needed investigative information, but she was no expert. If she couldn't manage to crack Aztec Chemical's System she felt sure that Chase's buddy at DEA could, as well as obtaining an order for wire-tapping for the executive office phone lines. Ashley thought tonight would be a good night to start surveillance so she really needed to hurry back and access her laptop. The sun beat down upon her as the steamy humid heat seemed to boil up off of the paved parking lot as she exited the cool confines of the personnel offices of Aztec Chemical Plant. The short sleeved black blazer she had slid on over her sleeveless white jumpsuit before entering the personnel office was clinging to her like a second skin by the time she crossed the paved parking lot to the space where she had parked the Jeep. Ashley peeled the blazer off and tossed it on the front seat as she canvassed the immediate area briefly making mental notes, before climbing in the Jeep.

CHAPTER FOUR

"Did you dispose of our little troublemaker like I requested?" drawled Adrianno Martinelli, puffing on an imported Cuban cigar while reclining in his executive leather chair behind a massive mahogany antique desk.

"Yes sir, he has been swimming with the fish in the D.C. river for about three weeks now, they may find the car but with the depth of those swift waters they will never recover his body as I had it weighted with concrete blocks and dumped from a barge about ten miles down the river from where we sent the car over the edge. You know I haven't let you down since you appointed me CEO of your operations four years ago, why now…. do you question my loyalty?" Victor Shayne silently crossed the thick plush burgundy carpet stopping like a predator mere inches from Adrianno's desk.

"My boy, if I doubted your loyalty there would

not be enough body bags or enough agents to cover the needed geographical area to recover all of your bits and pieces." Martinelli gave an evil smirk.

"Then we need to discuss the next order of business." Victor unflinchingly replied. "The dual shipments of cocaine and heroin will be leaving Columbia headed for the states this week. There will be numerous tons involved. This is the largest shipment we have ever obtained at one time. Which port warehouses have you selected to handle this kind of volume?" Victor walked over to original oil by *Leonardo de Vinci* admiring the million dollar piece of art. He stopped being amazed at the material things the wealthy spent billions of dollars on after spending the past four years abroad. Just the Italian marble in the adjoining bathroom suite cost more than one hundred thousand to be shipped into the country. Martinelli hadn't liked the pattern and quality of the first shipment of marble so it was returned and another was shipped with each individual piece wrapped in velvet then bubble wrap. Hunter green silk drapes shrouded each window, layer upon layer to eliminate the reflection of sunlight from entering the dungeon interior.

"I haven't decided yet, on which warehouses. You will be the first one to know when I decide. You can coordinate the transfer quickly I assume. This is the first time I have trusted you to distribute my precious cargo, don't disappoint me Victor. You know what happens when I become disappointed." Martinelli intently watched the circular pattern of cigar smoke spiraling upward.

The intercom blared suddenly on Martinellis' desk.

"Mr. Martinelli, I have an urgent call for you from Mr. Forcont at the Mustang Ranch in Nevada." The receptionist asked if he could take the call.

Martinelli holds one finger up, indicating for Victor to wait as he takes the call.

"Yes, Forcont. What can I do for you?" "Okay, that will be a sufficient amount, and delivery will be scheduled pending funds wired to my offshore account." "Tell Fox I said hello and our next meeting will be the tenth of next month at the Mustang Ranch in Nevada and not the Foxfire in Florida due to some renovation issues." Martinelli puts his cigar down. "I will transfer you back to my receptionist for the necessary account numbers you will need." Martinelli transfers the call back to his receptionist, barks a few orders before terminating the call then turns his attention back to Victor.

"Just let me know where and when the cargo will be arriving and I will take care of matters from there. I know every warehouse you have and how much each will hold. I know who will receive individual shipments and the amounts for each of them, and more importantly I know the cash value to be secured from each buyer and the offshore accounts to which the funds will be wire transferred. All I need from you is the when and where." With that Victor abruptly turned on his heel and headed toward the heavy mahogany door as it quickly swung open.

"Victor, fancy seeing you here." Candy purred, swaying her hips back and forth and leaning forward to expose even more of her half exposed breasts while undressing Victor with her eyes. Candy silently noted how his tall, muscular, sexy body seemed to be too confined in his Armani suit. His clean cut dark hair crowned his immaculately shaped head containing the most awesome devilish dark eyes and sensuous mouth she had ever seen. Candy would love to run her lips across his meticulously manicured beard and mustache as well as some other body parts, the man screamed out with extreme sex appeal. No matter how many advances she had made toward the man, he always brushed her off. She sauntered over to her daddy pouting as Victor ignored her blatant seductive attempts. "Daddy, could I have use of your yacht for the next two weeks?" "You know my husband is out of the country and the girls and I want to have a little fun."

Candy was an appropriate name for her, Victor mused to himself. For he was sure that daddy's money had supported Candy in packing massive amounts of *white powder* candy up her nose.

"Sure thing Candy Baby." Martinelli opened one the desk drawers and extracted a set of keys. "Have a good time, but be careful. I don't want another overseas call like the last time, advising me my yacht has been seized in a drug raid!" He told his daughter while dropping the keys into her extended palm.

"I will daddy. Don't you want to send Victor with me to protect me?"

"I don't think I can spare him at the moment sweetheart, this is his first trip to the states. Maybe, next time." Martinelli smiled threateningly at Victor.

"If nothing further is needed of me, I have business to attend to. I will be in touch with you in the morning." With that Victor exited leaving the little piranha with her daddy.

Once outside the executive office suites Victor drew the fresh salty sea air into his lungs. It felt so good to be back in Florida, he had been gone far too long. It had taken four years to work his way up to head executive of the Martinelli Cartel Empire. Victor was now privy to knowledge that had cost many men their lives. He seldom thought about what his life could have been like, to come home to that someone special; to maybe own a home, have children……. "Enough of that" he told himself, he was not a home in the suburbs-white picket fence type of guy. Maybe it was not such a good idea to be back in Florida, it was after all; the source of many unsettling thoughts, and if nothing else he prided himself in his ability to remain detached and show minuscule emotions. He had a job to do and that was what he intended on doing, and the end result was worth any risk that might present itself. He would simply complete the task at hand and get the hell out of Florida once and for all. Victor had reached the parking garage adjacent to the executive suite and motioned for his limo driver to circle around and pick him up. The long black limousine driver quickly observed Victor's command and within seconds was parked curbside. Victor eased his long lean frame into the cool comforts of the limousine.

"Where to Mr. Victor?" the limousine driver inquired.

"I need to go to the chemical plant warehouse in St. Andrews."

"Yes, sir. It should take about an hour to get there." The limousine driver closed the window leaving

Victor to his own devices for the duration of the trip.

Victor had suggested that Martinelli move a portion of the corporate offices for Aztec Chemical Plants to St. Andrews, Florida. This suggestion was simply to get the Martinelli Cartel within the jurisdictional limits of the United States Feds. Victor never expected Martinelli to agree. He had spent so much time abroad handling cartel business that it had been a real surprise that the merger and relocation to St. Andrews, Florida had already taken place. He had spent years performing unthinkable acts to prove his allegiance to the Martinelli cause. It was ironic that Victor was being summoned back to Florida, especially Northern Florida. His only conclusion was that some evil sea god must be playing a trick on him. It just simply did not make any sense. He needed to get a look at the plant and warehouse in St. Andrews, maybe that would explain some of the questions he had running through his head. He vaguely remembered the area from years earlier, but needed specifics. Besides the St. Andrews Warehouse was the only one of the Martinelli properties that he had not personally visited on-site at some point. He hadn't been in this part of the country for years. Victor glanced out the window of the limo as the Interstate gave way to the coastal highway and sat back to enjoy the breathtaking display of blue green ocean water. The sun was shining so brightly against the surface of the water it looked like glass, beckoning one to glide across its surface. An occasional pelican would dip its long black beak into the water and pull out its lunch for the day. The beach was dotted with bright blue and yellow chaise loungers, their occupants tanning their bodies while sipping a variety of frothy drinks with little umbrellas hanging onto the edge of the glass. Teenagers were soaking up the sun while walking along the edge of the shore as a couple of children threw a Frisbee for a black Labrador.

Victor broodingly took out a glass, dropped in a few cubes of ice, and then filled it to the top with good old *Jack Daniels*. He took several drinks before swishing the amber liquid around in the glass, watching the ice swirl around in its darkness. It was strange how the little solid cold blocks of ice could dissolve so rapidly against the warm bourbon whiskey. He knew a woman once that could dissolve him that quickly, melting away all his coldness with just the warmth of her silky hot body. He had yet to meet another woman that could make him feel that alive and human, and there had been many women.

Victor remembered once they had danced naked under the moonlight by the seashore. The water was fabulous and they had hung out for hours with only the moons glow illuminating their naked bodies.

"You're gorgeous," he had whispered, pulling her into his arms as she had surfaced from the glistening water like a sea-nymph. Water had streamed off her full perky breasts and down to her narrow waist above her long sexy legs.

She had been spellbound by his exquisite body and laughed down at him, her fingers tracing his rippling abdomen like a blind person reading Braille. With a somewhat urgent moan he had smoothed back the silky wet tendrils of her hair from her face, kissing her face, lips and gently sucking her breasts until the scorching heat and steady throbbing built up between her legs and she begged for release. She had stroked her hands through his long black hair before putting them on his shoulders and wrapping her legs around his waist. "I just wish this moment would never end." she had breathlessly sighed as her hand went down to stroke his long hard erection before sliding it into her hot wanton body. He kissed her neck, watching her nipples peak beneath his fingers as the sensations came again and again to wash over her as he took turns placing each taunt bud in his mouth sucking gently as she moaned and writhed with pleasure. He took her wrists and pinned them to her sides as his tongue and lips lifted her higher and higher into a sweet sexual vortex. Lightening hot desire flowed from her secret inner core before they both reached the ultimate climax. He had moved faster and harder and deeper until they both reached that point of no return, as she screamed his name over and over. They had become one that night, as one body, one soul with the sea washing all over them.

"I love you with all my heart and soul." she proclaimed with tears glistening in eyes the color of the ocean, reflecting like diamonds in the moonlight. "Promise me that this love will never end."

"Never, is a very long time." his voice suddenly grew husky as he tilted her chin up and stroked her long raven hair, his eyes glittering as a slow smile acknowledged her passion, reveled in it and promised much, much more.

"Mr. Victor, Mr. Victor, MR. VICTOR." the limousine driver said louder and louder.

"Sorry, my man. I guess I was daydreaming a little. What did you say?" Victor quickly fought to regain his composure.

"I asked back or front entrance? We are at the chemical plant warehouse." The limo driver was staring at Victor as if he were an alien from outer space.

"The rear dockside entrance will be fine." Victor had to restore his pulse rate back to normal. Just thinking about that woman had given him a raging hard-on like a teenager. This was not good, the woman was pure lethal even when he had not seen her in years. She had driven him crazy when they were together and coming back here brought all of the memories back that he had succeeded in pushing totally out of his mind. It was okay for him to lie to himself and say that he had not thought of her in the past five years for he was the only one that would know it was a lie. He reached for a cherry flavored cigar and drew heavily on its fine Cuban tobacco. Victor rarely smoked but this was an exception, he needed something to release the tension racking his body.

Victor exited the limo and walked to the rear entrance of the warehouse. He walked the perimeter noting several points of entry and exits throughout the entire facility. Pulling a small notepad from the breast pocket of his jacket, he scribbled several numbers down mentally calculating the distance from the docks to the main warehouse rear door. Frowning slightly he quickly drew a diagram indicating the placement of hypothetical boats. Four boats could safely slip into the port under the cover of darkness without drawing undue attention. An estimated sixteen men, four per boat would be needed to quickly offload the cargo into the warehouse; they could rotate as the next sequence of four arrived. Victor estimated the time frame somewhere between forty-five minutes and an hour and twenty minutes. The outer gates could be secured to prohibit any unwanted surprises. He also made a notation that from eight pm until eight am there were only two security guards on duty. SWAT members could take those two over with replacements before their shift started. It was Wednesday night, if Victor's calculation were correct, taking into account the time it would take to come from South America; Martinelli would have already made arrangements for the shipments to come in late Friday night. Paramount among his problems was the fact that Martinelli would not give him confirmation until Thursday at the earliest. That left very little precious time to coordinate an operation of this magnitude. Victor had suggested St. Andrews for personal reasons and now he knew why Martinelli had transferred his corporate offices to this plant in St. Andrews. The geography said it all. Out of all the properties that Martinelli had acquired this one held more ocean frontage than any other, and isolated at that. The ocean frontage was located at the back of the plant where the huge warehouses were strategically placed. The whole shipment could actually come into port right here. His plan was working out perfectly. He was left with no alternative but to contact Mr. Jones. After five long years, he was still not sure he was prepared for the ramifications of his actions. His only consolation would be the ensured safety of the one and only person he had ever truly loved, that and extreme justice for those who had lost their lives trying to make the world a better place. Did he just say "loved." Victor cursed to himself; he must be losing his mind. "Love" was not in his vocabulary, cared for, maybe, but love. No, absolutely not, he always had and always would be a love 'em and leave 'em kind of guy.

Victor climbed back into the cool confines of the luxurious limousine. He opened the glass separating the front compartment from the rear passenger suite of the limo. "Take me back to my hotel." Victor smiled realizing his words had awakened the driver.

"Yes, sir. Sorry I dozed off."

"No, problem." Victor remembered starting out

with Martinelli years ago as a driver. There were many times he had catnapped while waiting hours on end for his passengers to return to the limo.

The sun was beginning to set casting shades of orange and yellow across the glassy sea waters. Only a few beachcombers still lounged lazily on the bleached white sands. Streaks of silver lightning jagged across the sky as ominous storm clouds brewed in the distance. One could tell it was definitely August in Florida by twenty five days of the month yielding scattered to severe thunderstorms. The rain everyday was the one thing he had not missed.

Victor thanked the driver, slipped a few large bills his way and exited the limo in front of the Grand Hotel. Bourbon on the rocks gently called his name from the downstairs lounge and grill. Jetlag had squashed his appetite but not his thirst.

"I'll have bourbon on the rocks." Scanning the few patrons, Victor took his drink and found a corner booth where his back would not be to the door. The Grand Hotel was far from the tourist trap of the beach and yet near enough to the city to be convenient. The Hotel had once been an old railroad depot, the historic L & N Railroad that had been converted into a hotel and restaurant in 1912. The actual train tracks still ran through the inlaid brick of the lobby with novelty shops and lounges strategically placed to catch a patron's eye during the registration process. The Grand was one of the old historical landmarks that had not been demolished with the progress of a growing city. Victor had not felt it would be safe to be seen in the city for fear of recognition. His appearance had changed greatly and it had been over five years since he had been in this area but it was better to play it safe. He quickly finished his drink and left the lounge in search of the pay phones. He surveyed the corridor in both directions before lifting the receiver and depositing the required coins. He could always have used one of his available throw away cell phones, but he simply preferred not to have to hang on to the things.

"Jones, Victor here. You need to arrange a meeting in the morning. You will need to call in the best of the CIA, FBI, DEA and US Customs. Also, if you can get a small team of Navy Seals and a SWAT Team; they can be utilized as well. I will provide everyone with a debriefing."

"Ten o'clock in the morning at the old abandoned airport out on the county line road." With that Mr. Jones hung up the phone.

Victor hung the phone back up and proceeded to the elevators. Ten o'clock in the morning - that would be Thursday morning. If his calculations were correct the operation would need to be ready for action and on stand-by for Friday night. That only gave him a little less than forty-eight hours for a hell of a lot to be accomplished. Once in his suite he checked for messages before walking over to the hotel windows to scan the view below. There was only one message from the limo driver letting him know he had left his cigars in the limo and if he wanted him to return with them, just to call. It was going to be a long and sleepless night, but that was nothing foreign to him.

The telephone conversation earlier between

Martinelli and the Forcont fellow from Mustang Ranch had him perplexed. And who was the Fox fellow. Victor had been out of the states handling the Martinelli operations abroad but those names were vaguely familiar. He remembered working undercover some ten years earlier on a case involving the murder of a professional athlete, prostitution and money laundering at the Mustang Ranch; they were unable to get them on anything but income tax evasion; like Al Capone, Victor smirked to himself. The Mustang Ranch was the first legal brothel in the United States and was known to be the meeting place for mafia and underground political leaders. It has been burnt, rebuilt, seized by the government, run by the government, and sold off to recover tax debts. The owner had owned the district attorney and the sheriff at one time. When indictments were handed down he had absconded to Brazil which provided him the protection of no extradition on capital charges, if he recalled correctly. The Mustang Ranch re-opened within months of all indictments by a new owner, a nephew. The connection to Martinelli escaped him for the moment as well as the identity of this Fox character. That happened when you worked so many people in so many different areas of the world. Oh, well… it would come back to him in time.

Victor had become accustomed to long and sleepless nights years ago, and what precious little sleep he obtained was haunted by the ghostlike images of an elusive, beautiful, dark haired vixen of a woman. It had haunted him because the one thing she demanded was love; and that he was unable to give. He had to admit the many lovely and gorgeous women he had been with over the years had done little to remove the dark haired temptress from his bloodstream. Victor stared down into the darkness of the night noting in particular how the full moon cast almost wicked illuminating shadows on the horizon. Was there such a thing as true love or was it just an elusive dream, one that emotionally challenged souls were drawn to, seeking its energy? Victor had no desire to contemplate these answers right now. He walked away from the window and headed to the shower to rinse away such absurd thoughts.

CHAPTER FIVE

Ashley arrived back at the cottage and immediately stripped off the damp white jumpsuit that was clinging to her body like a second skin. She quickly showered, pulled on a pair of jean shorts and sleeveless lemon yellow button-up top before spending the remainder of the afternoon on the laptop and going through notes and case files. Ashley browsed the internet for related articles on cartel and mafia movement in the southern districts as well as accessing her Interpol account. She had set up the fax at the cottage and hooked it up to the spare phone line after contacting Uncle Morgan to fax some requested files down to her. Ashley was so excited when her uncle called her back to inform her that Lynn had located Patrick's photo ID from Aztec

Chemical and that the bodyguard Vince had made arrangements to courier it to her so that she would have it in hand by midnight tonight. Ashley had immediately left Chase a message with these details. She had spent hours hacking into the Chemical Plants Corporate Computer and had finally gained access. Chase was going to kill her for using her laptop and not waiting for the one he was bringing over later tonight but, time was of the essence. Martinelli was definitely using the Chemical Companies he owned as nothing but laundry mats for washing drug money, while transferring funds to overseas accounts. It was all in the files and corporate records she had accessed. Now all she had to do was prove it. The information she had obtained through hacking into the corporate files was not gained legally and circumstantial therefore, could not be used to obtain a search warrant. It was useful information at best but she needed something more concrete for her and Chase to go to the DA and get a search warrant for an entire warehouse that covered half a mile in width and all ocean front at that. She really needed Patrick's ID. According to the personnel records Patrick was still currently employed and received bi-weekly payroll checks that were being direct deposited into his account in D.C. Since this was the case, Ashley felt it was safe to assume that the magnetic strip on his ID for security access had not yet been deactivated. This also meant that Martinelli had something to do with Patrick's disappearance, which coupled with the tap on the Governors phone. That part really troubled her; hopefully Patrick was still alive or would be until the Cartel major shipments arrived. She needed to access the plant after midnight tonight to determine when and where the shipment would arrive and hopefully find Patrick alive.

Alone, in the den, a cold soda in her hand, Ashley stood at the open window and watched the surf beating the sandy shores on the beach below. The steady pounding of the waves and the heady scent of the salty air through the open window combined to steady her frayed nerves. Her favorite quote came to mind again; *The past is lost in a sea of darkness forever and the future is but a faint glimpse on the horizon.*

In a twelve year span; Ashley had faced drug-crazed addicts, murderers, rapists, drug dealers, smugglers, and gun runners. She had stared down the barrel of a loaded .357, a 9mm, a double barrel shotgun, caught the tip of a sword behind her ear, had her left hand busted with a crow bar, cut twice and been bitten on the arm by a Colombian drug dealers Doberman. She'd been thrown thirty feet from the blast of a meth-lab explosion and ended up walking away from that one with only a few cracked ribs and some minor cuts and bruises. She had been beaten and left in the woods to die when she had been burnt in an undercover operation that went bad; she could still remember the bloodhound that found her, licking her face. That was the last thing she remembered about that operation before waking up in the hospital. She had been in a coma for weeks after the Martinelli house exploded when serving warrants for the drug raid round-up from "Operation Sunburn," and had watched several officers die before her eyes, not to mention the eight SWAT team members ambushed that same night; *Jaded Justice* at its best.

What she'd never experienced before was this gnawing, gut wrenching anxiety that something catastrophic was about to happen, and not having a clue what it would be. She had called her Aunt Lynn to check on A. J. twice already today and had been assured that he was fine. Vince was guarding them all twenty-four seven. Maybe she had just been out of criminal work too long. She had spent the last five years building up her civil case work and avoiding criminal cases at all costs. Ashley was worried about Patrick's safety but that wasn't the cause of her unrest. She simply couldn't put her finger on it but she was sure she would soon. Trouble always had a way of finding her and she was sure tonight would be no different.

She flipped her phone open to make one more call to her office in D.C.

"Cameron Investigations." the pleasant voice answered.

"Hey red, how is everything going up there?" she asked.

"Ashley, you know I hate it when you call me red.

We have been busy, took another case. Josiah Hampton retained us for twenty five thousand dollars to recover his six year old daughter that has been kidnapped by his crack whore ex-wife. Larry is hot on their trail now. He will probably be flying out to Wyoming to get the child and bring her back here tomorrow." Gina Rae said.

"I remember his last case. We handled the investigation for his divorce several years ago. Tell Larry to be careful, Josiah's ex is a nut case, she stabbed him six times when he filed for divorce and custody." Ashley said.

"Sure, we've got it covered. How are things going in Florida? I still can't believe you are back in Bay City.

Ashley laughed. "I can't believe it myself. We are working all the leads we can find, that is our best course of action right now."

"Are you okay? Gina Rae asked.

"Sure, just jet lag and nerves. I miss all of you. Would you check on Aunt Lynn and A.J. for me? She wanted to cry and swallowed down the impulse.

"Consider it done. Keep your chin up, shoot

straight and we'll see you soon."

"Okay, girl. I've got to go. Take care." Ashley clicked the phone shut and stared out the window and the beautiful ocean.

Ashley's gaze was torn from the view of the surf to the sand being thrown up by a vehicle speeding up the pathway to the cottage. Did she lock the outer security gate? She was sure that she did. Ashley grabbed her gun but before she could panic the sleek green Jaguar tore up the drive and came to a screeching halt. Oh no! She had turned her cell phone off at the Chemical Plant earlier today and had forgotten to turn it back on.

"Where the hell have you been? What the hell did you mean going to Aztec Chemicals? Chase demanded, busting through the front door.

"I think you just asked a question and answered it with another question." Ashley calmly responded.

"You know what I mean. Are you trying to come back here and get yourself killed?" Chase snorted, stomping through the den to the kitchen like an enraged bull.

She followed him into the kitchen, intentionally not noticing how irate he looked, instead forcing herself to note the fact that he was just concerned about her welfare. No doubt, due to lots of past practices from their working together for years, Ashley had become numb to Chase's outbursts.

Raising her eyebrows, she lifted her chin and forced calmness into her voice. "I suppose I'd better fill you in. If I don't your blood pressure will continue to go up and you'll stroke out on me." She pulled two cold sodas from the refrigerator and motioned for Chase to join her on the deck. In unison she and Chase both pulled their patio chairs where the backs were facing the sliding glass doors, so they were looking out over the ocean. Ashley lit a cigarette, inhaled deeply and began to relay all the information she had discovered to Chase. She could tell he was angry by the furrowing around his brows and the occasional flaring of his nostrils; but he continued to listen without interrupting until she was finished.

"You know you lost two of my agents this

afternoon. They are both in training and were pretty embarrassed that some "dame" as they put it had given them the shaft. I knew at lunch that you were up to something so I had a couple of them follow you. I figured you would lose one so I sent two. You are still pretty damn good." His lips twitched in agitation.

"Thanks." A crease formed between her brows as she flicked the ashes from her burning cigarette into the lobster shaped ashtray on the patio table.

Lowering his voice he said, "The problem is, Ashley we are dealing with probably the largest drug shipment the states has ever seen. I know you are very good, always was and always will be. But, this is one case that none of us needs to be out solo on. I will hang around here and we can go over all your notes and files again. And at midnight you and I along with some other agents will go back out to the Chemical Plant utilizing Patrick's ID for you to snoop around, but you cannot go alone. "What exactly are you looking for?"

Ashley quickly mulled over his offer, and just as quickly decided to accept. She really had no desire to go solo on this one. There would be safety for all of them in numbers.

"I would like to get a look at Patrick's office. I discovered from his corporate e-mail account that he had just been doing a marketing spread on the new corporate office at St. Andrews, Florida. I think he came across something that he should not have at the plant. I pulled the specs from the property appraiser website for the Aztec Plant and have studied the layout and I think I can access Patrick's Office at the Aztec Plant. I need to gain access to the hard-drive on his computer to see if he documented anything we can use to locate him and bring down Martinelli. It appears there is going to be a very large shipment coming in soon. I noticed invoicing for several thousand *empty* chemical containers due to arrive at the St. Andrews Plant on Thursday morning. These are those high dollar stealth containers I told you about earlier. I think they will probably utilize these to store and ship the drugs on out to designated locations. What better location than Aztec's St. Andrews Plant due to the massive length of waterfront and the close proximity of the warehouse to the docks, plus the old airstrip which is no longer in use. It would be perfect if some of the cargo needs to be flown out of the country."

Understanding dawned, and Chase's eyes lit up. "Ashley, this is all fitting together. I received a call today from the Director of the CIA. He requested our attendance at a meeting at ten o'clock in the morning - Thursday. The meeting is to include; CIA, DEA, FBI, ATF, US Customs and a Navy Seal Team. DEA Director Madison has assigned you to go as well, he said with your past experience and Intel we could use all seasoned personnel we could get. I bet they have someone on the inside and the shipment is expected soon. Are you all right, Ash?"

She cleared her throat and forced her lips to move. "Yes, I just promised myself I would come down here to locate Patrick safely and return to D.C. quickly. I had no intention of getting involved in a drug smuggling raid or bust or working for DEA again. Twelve years of working narcotics cost me enough a long time ago. It is not something I want to relive," she said with a forced smile.

He looked into her eyes and saw the pain left there by Anthony. Somehow he suspected she would never truly recover from that relationship. It was almost like she held on to Anthony's memory like a lifeline, one that she would die, if she let go. And it wasn't just because of their son; she had always been that way by Anthony. He was really her one and true only love, her soul mate. He and Brenda had tried to fix her up on dates the few times she had visited them and they had visited her in D.C. Chase knew people everywhere since he worked all over for the government but Ashley never responded or showed anything remotely categorized as interest only offering each a minimal friendship at best.

At nine forty five they decided to head into town for something to eat and then meet the courier at the DEA Office by ten forty five. They secured the cottage and headed down the sandy path to the Jaguar.

"Oh, he definitely sounds like the boss for the Colombian Drug Cartel," Ashley said an hour later over drinks after their meal at *Joe's*, a local bar and grill. "How long has Martinelli been in town this trip?"

Chase hesitated. "About four weeks; it's not that difficult to explain. I guess I am surprised that we didn't figure it out sooner. Martinelli arrived here around the time Patrick went missing. I am sure it is not a coincidence either. What else?"

Ashley nearly spewed out a mouthful of margarita. Good grief, why hadn't she picked up on the time frames? But she didn't know when Martinelli came and went. "Has DEA been monitoring the Cartel movements, and do we have any idea who the mafia connection is locally?"

"Yes, ma'am, for four years now, and no we are not sure about the mafia link." Chase's face suddenly became an unreadable mask.

"Okay, what's wrong with you?" she asked.

"Nothing." Chase frowned. "We have spent a lot of manpower and hours chasing this one asshole all around the world. I hope we can finally take him and the whole cartel down once and for all. You know we still have active murder warrants out for his son, Ricky

Martinelli. His daddy obviously shipped him out of the country. We have been unable to locate him. There was even an airing on *America's Most Wanted* a couple of years ago." Chase settled back to finish his drink.

"We will get them." Ashley glanced down at her wristwatch and noted it was ten thirty. "We should probably pay our tab and head to your office to meet the courier. Then we still have almost an hour drive to get to the Chemical Plant; less than an hour the way you drive. Who will be going with us?" Ashley laid some bills on the table and motioned for the waitress to bring them their bill.

"My assistant Pete is definitely going with us and I asked Andy Gonzales, a DA Investigator to come along just to keep our legal and chain of custody issues in tact in case we find something. Gonzales can get a search warrant quicker than anyone else I know. Two other DEA Agents will be coming along; you haven't met Grayson or Roberto. We will all do a quick debriefing at my office. They are to meet us there at midnight. I felt sure we would have met with the courier and picked up your package in time for the meeting. We can decide who will go in and who will pull surveillance on the outside. The maps of the plant that you provided will be an asset. You don't need to use your laptop to access the Aztec files again, you know that it is not secure."

Ashley simply nodded a compliant acknowledgment as she climbed into the passenger side of the Jaguar. The street lights reflected brightly against the dark green exterior of the powerful machine. She looked out at the night sky filled with twinkling stars and one of the most beautiful full moons she had ever seen, dark clouds were beginning to roll in from the west. She and Tony both had an affinity with full moons. Annoyance seized her insides at his intrusive memory.

The streets were narrower than Ashley remembered. Quite a few businesses had popped up taking up the openness of the coastal right of ways. Ashley read the sign as they entered back into the city limits, "Welcome to Bay City - Home of the World's Largest Lobster." It seemed that Bay City was indeed a small growing metropolis from what had once been a unique seaside village. All things that were quaint and unique had a way of changing. Like Anthony, sworn to protect and serve as an officer of the law; then to just vanish in thin air. He left behind every ounce of integrity he had once lived by. The irresistible bad boy image he portrayed was only a camouflage for the gentle passionate man that lay beneath, or was it? She was so confused. She had lived on dreams and memories for so long now. Maybe it was time to truly let go of Anthony's memory. It wasn't like he had taken her virginity or forced her to do anything that she had not been the willing partner, she had been more the instigator. That was part of the problem; she was always more than willing to accompany Anthony to even the highest stakes possible. It was like her mind was playing a horrible conspiracy against her heart. She and Anthony were made from the same mold; they would have either killed each other or loved each other to greater heights touched by no other. Either way they had been doomed.

There had been others before him, all bad. One was a plant from the New Orleans mafia, that idiot burnt down her family home; another was a cop that she discovered later was on the payroll for the Dixie Mafia, and there was the good looking South Florida boy that just would not work. She had to admit, she had a terrible track record with men.

Ashley waited in the double parked Jaguar as Chase entered the federal building to pick up the courier package. She used her cell phone to call and check on A. J. before it was too late for her to do so. She smiled into the slender phones mouthpiece at A. J.'s excited jabber. He had been riding horses today and Leo the oldest of the quarter horses had bit Uncle Morgan in the butt. A. J. giggled that Leo was trying to get the sugar cubes out of Uncle Morgan's pocket. Uncle Morgan wasn't getting the cubes out quick enough to make Leo happy, so Leo bit him in the butt. Her son had elaborated to say that Aunt Lynn had laughed and said that Leo was always right and something "yuk" like Uncle Morgan had a cute butt. Aunt Lynn had offered to ice down Uncle Morgan's butt like she did for the horses when they had boo-boos and Uncle Morgan had muttered a couple of very "bad" words, to which A. J. had informed them that Uncle Morgan needed a spanking but it could wait until the boo-boo on his butt got better. Ashley told her son she loved him and clicked the phone shut. Chase found her laughing hysterically when he returned to the car with the package.

"What the hell is wrong with you? Have you lost your mind?" Chase stared at her as if she were some mental ward patient that had escaped and emerged in his vehicle while he was away.

Ashley recovered enough to relay the episode to Chase who laughed in turn.

"He is just like his mother, what comes up - comes out." Chase ignored the teasing slap to the side of his head as Ashley scowled at him for his comment.

"We have enough time for me to take you home and you can shower and change before the stakeout tonight if you would like to? It will be a very long night." Chase was already pulling the Jaguar out into traffic headed back to the beach cottage as he spoke.

Neither of them talked very much on the drive

back to the beach cottage, both absorbed in the night's upcoming events. They were both remembering how quickly a situation could become chaotic, deadly and out of control.

"Chase, I can let myself into the cottage." Ashley advised as Chase keyed numbers into the keypad and the electronic gates opened up revealing a dark two story cottage, she had forgotten to leave lights on inside.

"I can come inside and check things out before I leave."

"That is not necessary. I just thought I left some lights on but, I guess it wasn't that dark when we left." Ashley stared at the cottage in concern.

Just as she was getting concerned the back outside motion lights flooded the decks with light, glistening off the water from the pool. She exited the vehicle and vaguely registered the calming sound of the surf below as she kissed Chase on the cheek.

"If you will call and let me know when you're on your way back, I will be waiting out front."

"Are you sure you don't want me to check the

.........."

"No, I can take care of everything, but thanks anyway. Ashley called back to Chase as she inserted the key to the cottage door.

Something was wrong; the door had given away too easily to have been locked. The door squeaked slightly as if it reopened by itself. She could have sworn she had left lights on. Maybe she should have let Chase come in with her. Ashley's skin shivered slightly as she felt for the light switch as she entered the confines of the darkened cottage. She froze when the flipped switch emitted no light and instinctively pressed her body up flat against the wall as her eyes became accustomed to the darkness. Just as she was opening her purse to slip out her small .38 Smith and Wesson revolver the hardwood floors at the entry way beside her gave a slight groan. She was enveloped in a vice-crunching grip. She blinked her eyes again and found an ominous face covered by a black ski mask within inches of her own face. And then a gloved hand clamped over her mouth as the man's arm slithered around her neck while the other slipped a gun out of his waistband and pressed the nose of the gun into the crevice just below her ribs. She could feel the cold steel through her clothes.

CHAPTER SIX

Panic pummeled into Ashley's chest like the fast beating of a tambourine. She tried to scream, but her assailant's hand tightly covered her mouth, her frantic sounds muffled against the leather glove he wore. She attempted to bite the large gloved fingers but could not sink her teeth through the material.

"What's your name?" The man's whiskey scented breath growled in her ear. "Why are you snooping around where you have no business?"

Ashley winced in pain as her assailant jammed the barrel of the gun further under her ribs.

"If you want to live a second longer; when I remove my hand from your mouth you better start spitting out some answers lady." her attacker drawled.

"What do you want?" she strived to keep her

voice calm and keep him talking.

"Well, I can think of a lot of things I want; Maybe you could be nice to me and I will kill you quickly," he said lowering his voice. "Only after I have had a little fun."

When hell freezes over, she thought. Still, she knew she had to try to keep the man calm.

He hesitated momentarily, and then he groaned and dragged his sloppy lips through the hole in the mask, across the side of her face, pulling at the shirt that she wore. "Honey, you are one hot number, I can think of better ways to make you talk." He drug the nose of the gun down between her breasts, ripping the buttons from her shirt.

"Let go of me." Ashley tried to twist away, but the man was strong and relentless. His arm tightened painfully like claws of steel around her throat, succeeding in cutting off all of her air as he jammed the nose of the gun further under her ribs.

"The fun can wait until I get some answers." he jeered.

Ashley squirmed in the man's grasp, unable to break free.

Her attacker slung her to the floor where she landed with a thud, for a moment his hand was away from her mouth. Hope burst inside her and she opened her mouth to scream but he quickly slapped his palm back into place. He didn't say a word as he dragged her across the carpet, while she kicked her legs hoping to connect with something. Fear seized her spine. She couldn't let him take her. She had to get to her purse that had slipped to the floor.

"What do you know about Martinelli?" the man snarled, as he removed his gloved hand once more.

"Who or what are you talking about?" she asked cautiously, refusing to let this man sense her fear.

"Okay bitch, cut the act and answer my question?" he hissed.

"What or who is this Martinelli you're asking about, I don't know what you mean?" she stalled for time, still gripping at her handbag which he had thrown her on top of, it had her gun inside. "I really think you have the wrong person."

"The owner of Aztec Chemicals, Mr. Adrianno Martinelli. What is your name?" he demanded.

"Christy." she lied, hoping to confuse him in case he really didn't already know her true identity. She didn't know how he got in the house, why none of the alarms had gone off, but his iron-tight grasp and purposeful movements made his intentions clear.

Adrenaline scorched through her veins. She kept kicking, trying to bite, and all the while sliding her left hand inside her purse until it gripped her pistol. Whoever this guy was, he was very strong.

"Christy what?"

"Christy Jones."

He shrugged and loosened his grip slightly. "Maybe I'll believe that, but Martinelli don't make mistakes." "Who do you work for?"

"An advertising company."

"Okay Lady, What Advertising Company?"

"Global Advertising. Ashley blurted out the only name she could think of quickly.

"I will ask you one last time, what is your interest in Aztec Chemicals?"

She sensed that time was running out. Thinking quickly she picked up her foot and with all her strength turned and jammed her knee into the man's crotch. Before she could break free and remove the gun from her handbag the man recovered.

Then with horrifying swiftness pain exploded in the side of her head as the man smashed the butt of the gun against her skull.

"You son of a bitch." Ashley screamed while holding the side of her head where blood was trickling down.

"Shut up or I will kill you right now." he said lowering his voice.

Ashley hesitated, felt her heart miss a beat. She knew she had to keep him distracted. She had to collect her thoughts but she felt so dizzy and light headed.

"Let me go!" Ashley gritted through clenched teeth, trying to keep talking to keep herself from passing out cold.

"Let her go." a steely voice said behind them.

Startled by the sound of another male's voice, the man's head whipped around. His eyes widened at the massive size of the man standing two feet behind him with the nose of a gun cocked and leveled right between his eyes. Instantly he released Ashley, preparing to level his gun and take out the man that had interrupted his plans.

"I'll kill you first then the little ………"

One then two shots were fired almost simultaneously. The intruder hit the floor with a loud thud, his unfinished threat hanging in thin air. Blood oozed from the gaping hole in his head and chest. Within seconds the assailant laid in a pool of blood.

Ashley smelled the burning scent of gunpowder in the air as she knelt down and felt for a pulse and finding none arose from the floor, somewhat unsteady on her feet. She looked down at her blood spattered shirt and glanced up at Chase. He stood still, every muscle tensed, with his hand still tightly gripping the just fired gun.

"Are you all right?" he asked her, his voice lethally

quiet and controlled, yet laced with an undertone of fury.

"I'm fine," she said slowly, glancing back and forth at him and the dead stranger on the floor. "Just a bump on the head."

Chase nodded, and holstered his gun. "I'm going to the kitchen to flip the switches on the electrical box to see if I can power this place back up. The back floodlights must be on a separate box since they are working. He may have cut the lines outside in order to bypass the alarm; watch him until I get back."

"He's dead, it's not like he's going to get up and run off!" Ashley tried for flippancy to relieve the hysteria and light headedness she was feeling.

Within seconds bright light streamed through the cottage. Ashley heard Chase on the phone, giving the address and advising them to have the coroner in route also. Chase moved quickly. Ashley didn't have time to assist. The dead stranger was flipped over on his side and disarmed. Chase began searching his pockets for identification.

"Just as I suspected, Ashley." He pulled a small

folded piece of paper from the man's pocket and handed it to her, noting the extent of her injuries as he did so.

She hesitated for a second before reading in thick black scrawled writing her physical description, the cottage address and two brief instructions:

1) find out what she knows

2) kill the bitch

Ashley paled and the small piece of paper went floating to the floor as a sudden thought made her breath catch in her throat, but she managed to gather up enough courage to act composed.

Shivering, she stood up straighter. "Nothing I can't handle. I have been through this and worse before, and you know it."

"Like hell you can!" He frowned noticing her head wound had gotten worse and a large amount of blood was now trickling down the side of her face. Chase thought quickly and decided to appease her to keep her talking as she had quite a gash on the side of her head. "Okay, maybe you can handle it. But you aren't going to do it alone. What were you thinking?"

"You know when that man had his gun stuck into my ribs and threatened to kill me; the only person I could think of was A. J. I knew I had to keep him talking or distracted until I could think of what to do next. Somehow, I knew you hadn't just driven away."

"Well, this might surprise you," Chase said evenly, "but most people think I don't follow orders very well. So, when you all but ordered me to leave…….. I had to stay. I drove down the drive a little way, locked the car and walked back up here. Besides, I knew you had left lights on when we left."

Chase reached down and picked up the small piece of paper and placed it on the wicker table for the cops to tag and bag as evidence when they arrived. He pulled out his cell phone and made another call, requesting an ambulance be sent as well. A moment later, they heard the sound of sirens. Flashing lights cast strobes of neon blue through the windows.

Ashley wasn't certain exactly what happened next. Why had Chase called for an ambulance to be sent, her attacker was dead so the coroner's office would take his body. Everything seemed so fuzzy.

An officer knocked on the open door, then shortly afterwards another officer simply entered the open door. Grayson and Roberto from DEA showed up momentarily. The officers searched the entire beach house, checking every room trying to ascertain the reason for the disturbance. The attendants from the coroner's office arrived. An empty stretcher was wheeled in; then rolled back out shortly with a black body bag.

Ashley had taken a step out onto the front deck to get some fresh air when a strange buzzing sound kept getting stronger and stronger in her ears, everything seemed so far away. She slid down the side of the deck before everything went black.

Hospital
Emergency Room

"Miss Cameron, Miss Cameron?" the unknown voice seemed so far away.

"You're a very lucky woman." Dr. Augusta, dressed in crisp blue scrubs, pushed his glasses further up the bridge of his nose as he gingerly checked the wound to the lower forepart of his patient's skull and forehead. "Looks like you've got a nasty head wound."

Since Chase had followed Ashley in the ambulance to the emergency room, his phone had rung constantly. He had made arrangements for the attacker's body to be taken to the morgue and no information released to the press. This was an ongoing investigation and everything needed to be kept as quite as possible. Grayson and Roberto were staying behind to give the place a once over, and wait for the Crime Scene Unit to arrive. Chase had called Brenda and asked her to meet them at the hospital. He had to immediately calm her hysterics and assured her that everyone was okay.

"Lucky is one thing I don't feel right now." She glanced around the emergency room, remembering what had happened and became a little more oriented. Her head was pounding like a drum.

"We should x-ray to be sure you have no

concussion, though." The balding doctor continued to stare at the wound to Ashley's head. "Can't be too careful, you know."

"That won't be necessary." Ashley shook her head, wished that she hadn't as the bolt of pain shot through her skull.

"So, Miss Cameron – the doctor slipped his glasses off and placed them in the pocket of his scrubs – along with your ability to apprehend felons, you also have X-ray vision and when did you get your PhD?"

"I'll be fine in the morning." she ignored his X-ray vision and PhD remarks.

"I'm sure you will." The doctor removed a prescription pad from the counter behind him. "In the meantime, you might want to take some pain medication, only after you have stayed awake for at least 8 hours. I recommend that you stay in the bed for several days."

"That's not possible. I need to complete my investigation and get back to D.C. right away."

Dr. Augusta ripped the prescription from his pad, and then handed it to Chase. "I don't see any signs of a concussion, but keep an eye on her, anyway. Dilation of the eyes, clammy skin, disorientation and confusion. Make sure she does not go to sleep for the 8 hour time frame."

"I will finish up all of Ashley's admission and discharge paperwork here and then go by and have the prescription filled at the 24-Hour Pharmacy near my office, go ahead and take her to our house. I will be along shortly." Chase told Brenda as soon as she walked into the treatment room of the ER.

Brenda put a hand out to stop Ashley when she lifted her legs and set them on the floor, but she ignored her warning. Brenda watched as her jaw tightened and her face went pale. The slow breath she exhaled pretty much said it all.

"Ashley, lean on me and I will help you into the wheelchair and get you out to my car." "You are staying with Chase and I tonight." Brenda reached over to the bedside table and picked up the damp washcloth and wiped the perspiration off of Ashley's face.

Ashley reached up and wrapped her arm around

Brenda's neck for support, holding her breath while waiting for her eyes to regain focus. "So what do you suggest that I do?"

"You will stay with us tonight; we can sit up and talk for a while. I'm sure Chase has a lot of work he can be doing from home. Don't worry, everything will be okay." Brenda had gotten Ashley in the wheelchair and was already wheeling her out of the hospital toward the exit doors of the emergency room, while Chase completed the necessary discharge paperwork for them.

"Ashley, who is your insurance carrier?" Chase called to her before she got completely through the exit doors.

At the sound of her name, Ashley whipped her head back around, which made the earth spin out of control again.

Definitely not a good thing.

"Where is my handbag?" Ashley asked in alarm, holding her head as she spoke to dull the throbbing pain from speaking. "It has my gun in it."

Chase held up her handbag. "I have it right

here." He said shaking his head.

"Just look inside my billfold and you will see my insurance card."

"It's as good as done!" Chase waved his two best ladies out the exit of the hospital.

CHAPTER SEVEN

"Ashley, you are not going on this stakeout tonight!" Chase shook his finger at Ashley before stomping off down the hallway of his home.

"Now Chase, calm down. The doctor said that Ashley needed to stay awake. Maybe she can just sit in the car........" Brenda said gently touching her husband's arm.

"Stay out of this Brenda. She almost got herself killed tonight, in case you have forgotten."

"Would you two stop arguing and talking about me as if I wasn't sitting here?" I am going on the stakeout and that is final." Ashley stood up and tried to stomp off in a rage but ended up grabbing her head with both hands. She quickly regained her composure and slowly ascended the stairs, hoping that splashing some cold water on her face would revive her quickly.

Hopefully Brenda had a shirt in her closet to replace the ripped, bloodstained one that she wore.

"I don't stand a chance against you two, do I?" Chase shot an irritated glance at his wife.

Brenda sauntered up to her husband and kissed him lightly on the lips. "Of course you don't but; we both love you. Just make sure nothing else happens to her tonight. She is trying to hide the pain, but she really is unsteady on her feet."

"I know which is precisely why I didn't want her going tonight. I will make sure she stays in the vehicle." He scanned his wife's face for several moments before a small smile spread across his lips. "I don't know why you put up with me, and I don't know what I'd do if you didn't. Go upstairs and check on her while I use the phone to make the final arrangements for meeting the rest of the team tonight."

Brenda found Ashley standing in her jeans and bra, rummaging through her closet looking for a shirt to wear. "I have a black t-shirt that has Craig's "sharks" ball team logo slashed across the front." Brenda slipped the t-shirt off the hanger and handed it to Ashley.

"I thought you might like something dark and comfortable for the stakeout tonight. You also have a pair of jeans and underwear you left here during your last visit, this way you can shower before you go back to work." Brenda gently hugged Ashley.

"Thank you so much. I threw my shirt in the bathroom garbage. A cool shower sounds wonderful."

"Well scoot, I will run downstairs and make some shrimp dip. We can all have a quick snack before you guys go to work. Craig is spending the night with a friend tonight, so he will not be home, which means I don't have to cook!" Brenda blew Ashley a kiss and vanished down the staircase.

Ashley gingerly rinsed her hair with the honeysuckle scented shampoo and stared as the bloodstained water flowed quickly down the drain. The cool water felt refreshing as she lathered her tired aching body with the matching honeysuckle bath gel. It was like déjà vu, this was not the first time she had watched her blood wash down the drain. She exited the shower, patted herself dry and slipped into the pink flimsy bra and matching scrap of lace that was supposed to be panties that Brenda had left lying on the bed. They were an impulsive buy when she and Brenda went shopping on her last visit. Ashley grimaced slightly while pulling the oversized t-shirt over her still slightly aching head. Brenda was so thoughtful, she had even left her a pair of low cut black socks to slip on before putting her sneakers back on her feet. Ashley returned to the bathroom and dared not glimpse her reflection in the mirror as she ran her fingers through her long dark hair, squeezing out what water remained before descending the stairs in search of her two best friends.

They didn't see her until she was almost at the little breakfast bar. Brenda reacted with a flinch of startled surprise, and as anyone who knew her could have predicted, disaster ensued. The nearly full wineglass that had been resting near her right hand toppled over as her fingers bumped into it. The red wine sloshed across the top of the white marbled counter top as Chase grabbed the glass before it crashed to the floor.

Ashley watched the entire process with fatalistic acceptance. "I'm so sorry, everyone is on edge and I feel that it is entirely my fault.

"Nonsense." muttered Chase. "It has just been a very long day and you know Brenda doesn't need any excuses to knock something over."

"You'd better be careful or you will get wine all over you," Brenda noted smiling.

"Don't you worry about it, sweetheart," Chase said with good humor. "Have another glass on the house," he secured a clean wine glass from the wet bar and poured the rich red liquid into the glass before handing it to his wife.

"Thank you, dear," she said, gratefully. Brenda then glanced at Ashley's pale face and Chase' drawn expression with extreme worry for both of them going on a stakeout tonight but, she had become accustomed to the stress and worry after so many years. They were both well trained agents and would return home safely. The events from earlier tonight were just catching up with her but; she knew she had to hide her feelings. She wanted them both concentrating on the job at hand not worrying about her falling apart at home.

"The guys are going to meet us down at the corner bar one exit up from the Martinelli Chemical Plant Warehouse, in about forty minutes. I felt that would be a safe place to hook up with them as everyone there will be drunk and not really paying much attention to their surroundings. Our computer tech expert from DEA will be with Pete. He should be able to secure the information about Patrick from the mainframe computer if we can gain access without causing suspicion." Chase popped a cracker topped with shrimp dip into his mouth.

Ashley opened the courier package that Chase had placed on the table earlier. She flicked through the contents and pulled out the security swipe card belonging to Patrick.

"He will need this" Ashley handed the card to Chase for safe keeping. Also, could you ask him to access the system and download the main gate entrance and exit logs for the past say, six weeks?

"Sure can," Chase continued munching on his

crackers.

"Also, if he can get the legend from the personnel files - this will give us a listing of every employee that has entered and the times they entered and left the premises." Ashley dipped a cracker in the bowl of shrimp dip and popped the delicious concoction into her mouth.

"Brenda your cooking is impeccable. I miss good food. Tony was pretty good on the grill; his steaks were to die for. Poor, A.J., I live out of cans and frozen boxes because I can burn rice!" Ashley laughed, which caused her to grimace slightly as a bolt of pain shot through her head.

"Well, we better hit the road if we plan to meet them on time." Chase leaned over and kissed Brenda on the lips while giving her butt a quick pat. "Lock up behind us."

"Make sure you guys are careful and I love you." Brenda leaned against the locked door as the duo exited through the garage.

Ashley slowly climbed into the passenger side of the Jaguar and slumped down in the seat, totally exhausted already. She truly hoped they came up with something useful tonight and that they all returned safely. The turn of events earlier in the night had really unsettled her nerves.

She glanced out at the passing vehicles as their headlights cast bright streams of light on everything they passed. Ashley shifted impatiently in her seat, automatically taking in the oceanfront atmosphere. She couldn't shake this uneasy feeling. Then she remembered the meeting that Chase had told her about, in the morning, wasn't it?

"Chase, didn't you tell me there is a meeting we have to be at in the morning?"

"Yes, at the old abandoned airport out on the edge of the county line. All the top dogs, the "who's who" from the cop world will be present. It has to be something really big to call all of us to a meeting on this short notice and to schedule the meeting out in the middle of nowhere.' Chase shook his head questioningly.

"I was just wondering; who did you say called the meeting?"

"Jones, Director of the CIA. Why?"

Ashley shifted uncomfortably in the car seat, "I was just curious who could pull a meeting of such magnitude together in such a short time frame."

"Like I said, it has to be something really big. We will find out in the morning. Right now, we need to concentrate on the business at hand. You and I will pull surveillance from outside the plant. Our computer geek is wired, so we can monitor everything he sees and hears."

"Why do you call him a geek? That is rude." Ashley admonished.

Chase laughed, "Well, he is." Chase gassed the Jaguar to pass an eighteen wheeler before swooping down the exit ramp toward the corner bar.

The parking lot of the Corner Bar was packed. Ashley looked through the Jags tinted windows at the varied license plates displayed on the patron's vehicles. Chase was pulling to the very back of the bar; the parking lot seemed like a football field.

"I bet a lot of drunks have lost their vehicles

here," Ashley noted aloud.

"I can assure you they have, myself being one of them!" Chase laughed; Brenda had to come and get me one night and find my car for me."

"I'll bet she was pissed."

"You know it; I paid for that one for months." Chase came to a stop in the very back of the parking lot, pulling up beside a black van. Pete approached their car as the driver's window was sliding down.

"Hey Ash, sorry about your trouble earlier tonight." "I secured the beach house when we finished collecting all the evidence. We left two of our men out there to guard the house in case you want to return later. There will be one of our guys inside and outside the place twenty-four-seven until we finish this case. You looked a mess earlier" Pete said unthinkingly.

"Thanks. You ought to see the dead guy," she smirked. She knew her face was bruised, swollen and the cut on her forehead and mouth still looked raw and painful.

"Let's pick up the pace here." Chase ordered,

handing the security swipe card to Pete. "Geek boy will need this to gain access to the plant. We'll cover the outside perimeter."

Chase spent a couple of minutes repeating to Pete what information they needed to secure from the inside, before shifting gears and tearing out of the parking lot ahead of the remaining officers.

The short drive to the Chemical Plant passed in heavy silence and Ashley waited impassively for the impending doom. She suddenly felt everything slipping away and didn't know how to stop it. Where was Patrick? Was he dead or alive? Would they be able to find the answers? It was up to her and Chase to make it happen.

They all assumed their positions as "geek boy" entered the facility under the pretense of removing a computer virus that was attacking the plants operating system.

Through a splitting headache, Ashley watched through night scope binoculars as Chase listened to the conversation through the tiny earphone he was holding up to his ear. After what seemed like an eternity the guard at the gate finally allowed "geek boy" admittance.

"Whew," Chase breathed a sigh of relief. "That was close, the guard wanted to call the CEO for approval when he received a call that one of the chemical treatment machines had malfunctioned and a small fire had broken out in Level 3, on the back side of the plant. I'll have to commend Pete for his excellent pyro-maniac timing."

"He set a fire?" Ashley asked, frowning.

He drew a long breath, his fingers tightening on the steering wheel. "It's working so far."

"Don't tell me, let me guess," Ashley got out sarcastically. "This is just another example of DEA routine practice, right? A few good old boys breaking the law just to enforce the law?"

Chase didn't look at her as he continued staring out the window at the guard gate. "No, as a matter of fact, this isn't routine. Believe it or not, Ashley, we really don't have a lot of city-type crime here anymore. Everyone still knows everyone to well for that. Occasionally we have a high-hitter arrive but nothing like

Martinelli since you left here before. It is strange that now that you are back, Martinelli is also."

"It is more than strange, it's criminal. I remember what he turned this area into before. I still wonder why he chose St. Andrews."

"Give "geek boy" some time and we may have that answer, he's only been inside for thirty minutes." Chase said glancing down at his watch.

"I certainly hope so." Ashley lifted her binoculars again and peered toward the warehouse, ignoring the shooting pain in her head. Sensing movement Ashley turned her binoculars toward the bay water. A small plane came down out of the sky, landing with a gentle soft hum on the water behind the warehouse. There was no time left now. The computer geek had to get out of the plant immediately.

"Chase, you have to get him out of there now." she managed, forcing a distant calm into her voice. "A floater plane just landed in the bay."

"Pete, pull everybody out now." Chase growled over the walkie instructing the team to abandon the operation.

"Chase, Look! He's coming out through the guard gate now." Ashley pointed through the darkness toward "geek boy" strolling casually out into the parking lot, briefcase in hand.

"Pete, pick him up and get everyone back to the office for debriefing." Chase slammed the Jag in reverse and slid out of the parking lot, never turning on the headlights.

"I wonder if "geek boy" came up with anything useful." Ashley mused.

"If anyone could, he could." Chase accelerated up the interstate ramp heading back to the DEA Office in Bay City.

They had been on the road for about fifteen minutes when the ringing musical sound of *As Time Goes By* denoted Chase' cell phone ringing.

"Yea, go ahead." Chase exchanged the walkie for the cell phone.

Ashley patiently waited for Chase to end the call, dying to know what was being said.

Chase finally clicked the cell closed. "He got everything we needed. Someone at Aztec Chemical Plant is definitely involved in the disappearance of Patrick, as they are still using his high security clearance account and password on the computer. According to the employee printouts, he hasn't missed a day's work in over a month."

Ashley sighed. She'd known, of course, that sooner or later they would have the information they needed. She just hoped this didn't mean that Patrick wasn't still alive.

"Something wrong?" When she didn't answer, just sat there slumped down in the seat. Chase thought she was sick. 'What's wrong, Ashley?"

"I - Patrick - ' She looked up, her solemn expression, quickly replaced by one of no expression whatsoever.

"He's a fighter like his uncle, I'm sure he's okay." Chase said, understanding the line of her thoughts. "Ashley." He leaned over toward her, clicking on the interior light. "You look extremely pale, Are you sure you're alright?"

"I'm just fine, Chase. Really." She smiled tightly at him. "It's been a very long stressful day, that's all. If you wouldn't mind, I'd like to close my eyes and rest, until we reach your office."

"No problem, doll, it hasn't been eight but it has been more than four hours." Chase clicked off the interior light and turned the car radio on very low, hoping that Ashley would actually sleep until they reached his office. She really looked exhausted but, neither he nor Brenda could convince her to just stay at home and wait.

Ashley stared out the window at the receding chemical plant and warehouse. She found herself staring up at the twinkling stars in the dark black sky for what seemed like the hundredth time in the past couple of days. She missed A. J, missed her home, and her simple private investigations business. There were some things she didn't like being uncertain about but, one thing was for sure. When this case was solved she would be on a plane going back home to a place with pleasant memories; unlike the tortured ones that lay on the horizon in this small coastal town in Florida. She closed her eyes to block out the memories for just a few minutes.

"Ashley, we're home." Chase gently tapped her on the arm.

"Home, I thought we were going to your office?"

"We did, about two hours ago. You were sleeping so well that I had one of the guys stay out in the car with you. He did say that you snored. I went inside and took care of all the paperwork for the stakeout. When I came back out to the car you were still asleep and here we are." Chase pointed to the garage of his house.

"You should have woke me up, and I don't snore!" Ashley grumbled, climbing out of the car and ringing the doorbell.

"Why are you ringing my doorbell, I live here!"

The door opened wide and a sleepy Brenda ushered Ashley in the house. "I kept some coffee warm for us." she said.

Three minutes later, Ashley and Chase sat at the breakfast bar. Brenda poured the ebony steaming liquid into the cups. She placed a saucer containing blueberry muffins in front of each of them before walking behind Chase and rubbing her husband's back.

"2:30 am," Ashley glanced down at her watch, savoring the last of her muffin.

"10:00 am will come very early." Chase yawned.

"I'm not sure if I will be able to sleep, but I will certainly try." Ashley sipped the last of the warm liquid from her cup. "Thanks, Brenda. The coffee and muffins were excellent." She stood up and kissed both Chase and Brenda on the cheek. "Can one of you take me to the beach cottage to change in the morning before we go to the meeting?"

"A couple of your bags are up in the spare bedroom. One of the guys brought them over while you guys were out on the stakeout." Brenda said yawning.

"Thanks again. I'm going to bed; I'll see you both in the morning."

"Goodnight." Chase and Brenda echoed in unison.

"Chase, I am really worried about Ashley."

Brenda voiced her troubling thought out loud once Ashley was out of earshot.

A tear slid down her cheek. Chase brushed it away with his thumb, his touch infinitely gentle and warm. His lips were equally gentle as he dipped his head and kissed his wife. He swept his tongue into her mouth.

When he finally broke the kiss, his eyes shone of love and tenderness. "I know hun, she is exhausted, hurt and just won't stop right now. She seems a little shell-shocked, everything will be okay."

"Okay," she agreed.

"Good." He stroked her cheek for a moment, then took a step back and held out his hand. "Shall we go to bed?"

Never taking her eyes off him, she placed her hand in his and said, "Yes."

CHAPTER EIGHT

Thursday morning came much too quickly. Ashley had taken the pills the doctor prescribed before going to bed and had surprisingly slept very well. The soft silk sheets and fluffy pillows had felt like a dream when she had slipped into the bed six hours earlier. She glanced over at the bedside clock, 8:35 am. Ashley had time for a quick shower before getting dressed. She really hated that she and Brenda hadn't been able to spend any time together. Maybe today would render a miracle and everything would be happily over.

Speaking of happiness, Ashley picked up the phone from the night stand and dialed her uncle's number.

"Hello." The phone was answered on the first ring.

"Aunt Lynn. It's Ashley. How are you guys doing this morning?"

"Good, A. J. is getting dressed to go to the stables. He loves Leo, says that he is going to take him home with him when you get back. He said Leo can have the spare bedroom."

Ashley laughed at the thought of a quarter horse sleeping in the spare bed. "I'm afraid Leo wouldn't enjoy living in a townhouse."

"Have you heard anything about Patrick yet?" Lynn's anxious voice questioned.

"Not yet. We obtained a few successful leads late last night. It looks very promising. As soon as I know something, you know I will call you and Uncle Morgan." Ashley promised.

"I know you will honey, we love you. Here's A. J., he is bouncing up and down wanting the phone."

"Good morning little man." Ashley eyes brimmed with tears of happiness at the cheerful sound of her son's voice. She missed him so much; this was the longest she had ever been away from him.

"Mornin Momma, I'm going to feed Leo. He wants to come and live in our spare room. That be okay?"

"No sweetie! Leo wouldn't be happy in such a small place. Maybe we can look for something bigger to buy; a place in the country where you can have several horses."

"But, Leo won't mind." pouted A. J.

"I know he wouldn't mind sweetie, but he would really like a bigger place to live; don't you think?"

"Okay, momma. I gotta go; Leo gets hungry early in the mornin. Aunt Lynn says that he eats more for me."

"Okay, I love you." Ashley made smacking kissing sounds over the phone.

"Aunt Lynn, we really are getting closer. I will let you know something just as soon as I know. I love you and Uncle Morgan. Make A. J. behave and take care. I will be in touch again soon."

"We love you too, sweetie, bye."

Ashley held the disconnected phone receiver in her hand listening to the dial tone for several seconds before replacing it on the hook. Dear Lord; let today be the answer to all their prayers. With that Ashley dressed in a fresh clean pair of faded jeans, with holes worn out in the knees. She abandoned the sleeveless sweater in favor of something she wouldn't have to pull over her head. She gingerly touched the wound on her forehead, it didn't hurt quite as bad as it did last night, but it looked horrible. The swelling was still present along with the appearance of dark purple bruising. Buttoning the silk cap sleeveless red top while brushing her hair took some talent, she grabbed a hair tie out of her bag and pulled the massive mounds of unruly waves loosely away from her face, trying to leave enough hair hanging down to camouflage her wounds. Ashley rummaged through the overnight bag before securing her red sandals and slipped them on her feet before glancing in the full length mirror. There were times when she wondered who the woman was that stared back at her. This morning she simply didn't have time to discuss this with herself; she brushed on some light red lipstick and walked toward the foyer which headed toward the stairs in search of Brenda and Chase.

 Ashley paused at the top of the staircase to

admire the huge fish tank against the wall at the top of the staircase. The bright colorful fish were zooming back and forth, and in and out of their ceramic caves nestled against the neon gravel bottom. This exotic element had to belong to Craig, he had always loved fish. She would have to find time to spend with him as well as Brenda before she left for D.C. Craig was after all her godson. She hadn't seen him since last summer when he stayed with her and A. J. in D.C. for Brenda and Chase to go on a cruise to the Bahamas.

Ashley heard Brenda's laughter just as she reached the landing of the stairs.

"Good morning, you got up early this morning." Brenda shoved a hot cup of coffee into Ashley's unresisting hands.

"I could say the same for you two considering you both beat me downstairs." Ashley sipped the warm brew with greed.

"We would have banged on your door and hastened your progress before too much longer." Chase glanced at his Rolex watch. "We need to leave in about fifteen minutes to make it to the county line airport by 10:00 am for the meeting; unless you want to do your usual and show up an hour late?" Chase mockingly smiled.

"Don't start your crap with me this morning, mister. I have been ready. And since when am I always an hour late?" Ashley huffed.

"Well, let me see. Do you want every time in the past fifteen years or just the past three days?"

"Okay, so I have a little problem with punctuality. There is no need for you to start your preaching. I am ready to go whenever you are."

"Go ahead and finish your coffee while I run upstairs. We will leave when I come back."

"Is he always this grouchy in the mornings?" Ashley asked Brenda when Chase was out of hearing range.

"I heard that." Chase yelled down the stairs.

Brenda laughed. "Voices carry - there is an echo up and down the stairs. And in answer to your question, he is actually quite mild this morning. Sometimes he can be a real bear."

"I'm so glad you're the one married to him. I am not a morning person. I would kill him." Ashley finished off the cup of coffee, rinsed the cup and placed it in the dishwasher.

"There are times I ask myself why I put up with his moods but, then I remember how much I love him. But, that doesn't mean that I don't want to kill him at times myself."

"Brenda, I want us to spend some time together as soon as we finish this case. I would love to see Craig too. I haven't even seen him since he stayed with us last summer. Remember a couple of years ago when A. J. killed three of your exotic fish because he took them out to "pet" them."

Brenda screeched with laughter. "I had totally forgotten about the fish escapade. But, Craig is sixteen now. You know, license - car. I don't see him very much anymore; he spends most of his time with his blonde bimbo girlfriend. Chase says that I won't like any girl that Craig dates, but honestly this girl is not for him. She has to know where Craig is every minute and if he even speaks to his friends that are girls, she cries and says that he is running around on her. A real drama queen that one is!" Brenda shook her head in exasperation.

"I hear Chase stomping down the stairs; you better get your purse and get ready to leave."

Ashley gave Brenda a quick hug and went to retrieve her purse from the table in the foyer.

As they were leaving the residential area of town, Ashley spotted several people out walking, most with their dogs. All the walkways were tidily trimmed and hosted beds of multi-colored flowers. Children were already splashing in a pool; balls, toys and swing sets littered the yards. Many waved as they passed by, a fact that they recognized Chase's Jaguar.

The old airport on county line road was miles from anywhere, literally in the middle of nowhere. Trendy downtown shops and architecturally impressive building lined streets had been lost thirty miles of road behind them.

"Are we ever going to get there?" Ashley sat

straighter in the seat peering out the windows at the vast nothing surrounding them.

"You've done really well, Ash. I'm surprised you haven't asked, "Are we there yet? Are we there yet?... at least a hundred times by now." Chase laughed.

"Okay, smart-ass. I have been here several times, years ago. But, I don't remember it being this far out." Ashley pointed out the window to the upcoming turn marked by an old rusty sign with an arrow pointing - County Airport. Chase quickly turned off the main paved road onto the narrow sandy lane.

"The old airport is still operating, but only for government usage. We hold special meetings in the conference room upstairs. It is only utilized for high profile operations. When we get there, just remember the inside looks a whole lot better than the outside of the building."

About four miles later, Ashley looked back and all that followed them was a long cloud of dry white sandy dirt kicked up by the high performance tires of the Jaguar. Long arms of asphalt runways, cracked and overcome with weeds were now visible. The long white block building appeared deserted behind the black iron fencing. It was a tall building with long sad looking windows, covered with wrought iron bars. She couldn't tell if the windows were covered in grime or if they had been dark tinted. Chase maneuvered the Jaguar around behind the fences to a large parking garage in the rear of the building. The lot was full of about twenty-five government vehicles.

"Chase, who all did you say was going to be present at this meeting?" Ashley swallowed hard, her throat suddenly bone dry.

"Jones, the Director for the CIA called the meeting. He advised me that CIA, DEA, FBI, ATF, US Customs, SWAT Team, and a Navy Seal Team would be present. Our DEA Director Madison will be present as well. I will bet you fifty bucks that it has something to do with Martinelli."

"Jones didn't tell you why the meeting was being called?"

"We never know the exact subject matter for

meetings out here. Oh by the way, the wire-tap at the Chemical Plant will be up and operating today, the judge signed the order last night."

"How did you get it done so quickly?" Ashley asked.

"Judge Thatcher is awesome, he still believes in the cause." Chase answered frankly.

"That is good to know. Maybe it will give us what we need. And, I remember Judge Thatcher. He has been on the bench for almost thirty years now. They don't come any more solid and honest than him." Ashley's butterflies vanished somewhat, and a little relief was apparent in her eyes.

"Well, are you going to sit in the car and miss all the fun?" Chase called back to Ashley as he exited the Jag.

Ashley slammed the door to the Jag with frustration and followed Chase up the cracked walkway to the rear steel door of the old airport. She had been out of criminal work too long. It simply made her nervous, and she still had a massive headache. That and the fact that she had been almost killed last night didn't help any....

Chase knocked once on the door and then held his badge up to the small octagon shaped window at the top. Within seconds the door was opened by Grayson.

"Hey, my man." Chase slapped Grayson on the back. "You remember Ashley.

"Glad to see you. I wasn't sure if you would make it today after all the excitement you had the past twenty four hours." Grayson extended his hand in greeting.

Ashley shook her head. "I'm fine." She self-consciously shifted her weight from one foot to the other and tightened her grip on the shoulder strap of the heavy handbag she carried. The weight of the gun in her purse uncomfortably reminded her of the assault last night.

"Roberto and I cleaned up the house and secured everything after the Crime Scene Unit left, while Chase went to the hospital with you. It is so clean you can't tell anything ever happened. We were sure worried about you, just glad you're okay." Grayson smiled and motioned for them to follow him down the corridor to the elevator.

"Grayson do we know what this meeting is all about yet?" Chase pushed the elevator button to take the trio to the second floor conference room.

"No, not yet. Everyone is here except the guy who is supposed to do the briefing. Jones said he hadn't arrived yet, go figure."

"Who is he, do you know?"

"Don't have a clue. I guess we will all find out what is going on in about five minutes." Grayson looked down at his watch.

Chase pushed the double doors open to the conference room and waited for Ashley to enter ahead of him.

Ashley scanned the room full of cops and recognized a few faces she knew. The drop down screen was already in place to present slides and a black cherry wooden podium stood off to the right in the front of the room. There were rows and rows of tables with chairs. She selected one in the very back of the room next to Roberto.

"Hey girl, I'm sure glad to see you vertical." Roberto patted the seat of the chair next to him.

Ashley took the seat he offered.

Director Madison approached the table where Ashley had taken a seat. "I am happy to see you are okay, young lady. You have a nasty bruise on your forehead. Are you sure you feel up to being here this morning?"

"Yes sir. I have a bit of a headache, but it actually looks much worse than it really is. Thanks for your concern." Ashley shook his offered hand.

"You were always one of my best agents. I am just glad to have you aboard for this one." Director Madison headed back up to take his seat in the front of the conference room.

"That is Mr. Jones, the Director of the CIA." Chase pointed to the short, gray haired elderly man with glasses that entered the front of the room a few minutes after they were seated. "And the tall, thin, bald headed man with round glasses that he is talking to is Mr. Lawrence, the director of the FBI.

"I know you are ready for me to inform each of

you what the special detail is this time. Without any further delay, I will allow our undercover operative of five years now to introduce himself and provide you with the definitive details." Mr. Jones pushed the small sliding panel door at the front of the conference room open and motioned for the speaker to enter.

Ashley checked out the tall handsome man's two-hundred dollar haircut that tapered over the ears and longer in the back, dark sideburns, meticulously cut mustache, and; his designer Armani suit. He had to be pushing 6'2" at least. An air of success and confidence oozed from his every movement. The planes of his face appeared steep around the dark sunglasses that hid his eyes. The line of his mouth looked hard, yet sensuous and vaguely familiar. Something must be wrong with her; she hadn't felt a sexual attraction for any man since……

The man removed his sunglasses and said two words before all hell broke loose. "Good morning."

"Son of a bitch!" Ashley yelled from the back of the conference room.

Every officer in the room yanked their head

around to see who would have the nerve to start cursing the speaker before he even got started. Chase knew exactly what was going on.

"Ashley, save it for later." Chase ground out through clenched teeth.

"Like hell, I will. Ashley stood up and stomped up to the front of the conference room until she was chest to ribcage with......

"ANTHONY Langston!" She heard his name spat out of her mouth like poisonous venom. Ashley was trembling inside with rage and some other emotion she would rather not even remotely consider at this point.

"Thank you miss. That will save me the time of introducing myself." The hard lines of Anthony's face cracked with a one sided smirk, at the same time threatening her to silence.

"No Ashley!" Chase called, headed in her direction. But before he could catch up with her, Ashley's right hand balled into a fist and she punched Anthony right in the nose. His hands went up as blood started trickling down in little droplets onto the expensive white silk shirt and burgundy tie beneath his jacket.

The room was full of the most elite officers of the law; but before Ashley could redeem herself; the man who had crushed her whole world over five years ago; turned to his fellow officer.

"I've got this one." With the same power he'd used to control her years earlier, Ashley was led out of the conference room and into an outer office which contained solid oak walls.

She tried for an elegant lift of her head. "You are a pompous, arrogant, self-centered, son of a bitch."

"Have a seat." Anthony indicated the worn chair by the desk.

"I don't want to have a seat. I want to kill you, you stupid ass."

"I said, have a seat." Anthony gently pushed Ashley into the seat. He popped one muscled hip on the desk's corner and smiled down at her.

His eyes alone could make a woman say yes.

She tightened her mouth, tightened her limbs. "Don't try to weasel out of this one by telling me you don't remember."

"Oh, I remember, alright."

His tone, spoke of honesty. This she could not accept. She shot him a narrow eyed look. "You're good but you're not that good. Try the look of honesty on someone who doesn't know you for the lying, egocentric jerk that you are."

He chuckled, the sound hitting her like a slap in the face.

Before she could stop herself, Ashley swung to slap Anthony in the face.

"Hell, no, you don't! Anthony successfully averted the intended slap. "Stay in that chair and close your mouth and listen to me."

"You're a lying skunk."

His expression showed no offense. "I did what was best for both of us at the time. I wasn't a nice guy; there were things that you didn't know; and things that I had to do."

"You weren't a nice guy at all, and a coward to boot."

He smiled wider, "Tell me exactly what you are the most pissed at me for?"

"You still want to be sitting here next year? That's about how long it would take." Ashley hissed.

"Ashley, listen to me. I have changed a lot; there were reasons for what I did."

"You haven't changed, Anthony. Leopards don't change their spots."

He studied her for a long moment. She was still the beautiful gorgeous creature he remembered; the one woman that had haunted his dreams nightly for five long years. He quickly masked the pain of the lost years by a steely expression.

Anthony sighed, rubbed one side of his head.

She stared at him. "You still do that?"

"What?"

"Rub the side of your head at your temple when you're frustrated."

"You've seen this move before?"

"I've seen all of your moves, Anthony!" She jerked upright, banging her knee on the corner of the desk. Anthony's hand reached over her shoulder to sit her back down in the chair.

Anthony reached in the breast pocket of his jacket and pulled out a crisp white monogrammed handkerchief and dabbed at the blood still dripping from his nose. "I'll give you this; you still have a good right hook."

She moved to get up again.

He took a long breath. "I do have handcuffs."

"Are you trying to ask me out on a date? You would have to use force, I certainly wouldn't go willingly. Been there and done more than that; once was enough!"

His eyes warned her that she was walking a fine line. She met his gaze, black eyes that rarely revealed any emotion.

He slid his hand up the nape of her neck and tilted her head gently backward. One finger softly tracing the laceration to her forehead and the swollen purplish bruising. "What happened to you?"

"None of your damn business!" She jerked her head away from his hand and winced slightly in pain. "What the hell are you doing here, anyway?"

"I have been undercover for the past five years working for the Adrianno Martinelli Drug Cartel under the name of Victor Shayne. That is why I am here today. I have less than 48 hours to disperse the information required to shut down his whole operation, and seize all his assets. That is why the best of the cops are here today. I had heard that you had gotten out of law enforcement years back, I guess I was misinformed?"

"The Director for DEA has sworn me back in on a temporary assignment. I am trying to locate my cousin Patrick Morgan." Ashley looked down so he wouldn't see the pain in her eyes, she didn't want to tell him any more than she had to and her personal reasons for being here were after all, none of his damn business.

Nothing in his eyes flickered sympathy. She was grateful. "Patrick is alive and well. The CIA have him under protective custody and you can't reveal that to a single person yet." His steely tone was low and soft but allowed for no argument.

She breathed a long sigh of relief and disbelief; then nodded her head in acknowledgment just as there was a knock on the door.

"Anthony, you have a whole room full of the best cops I could find. We need to get this show on the road." Director Jones' command gave no room for hesitation.

"Yes, sir. We are on our way in now."

Anthony held the door open for Ashley to exit the outer office and leaned down placing his mouth next to her ear. "We will talk after the debriefing."

Ashley marched down the short hall toward the main conference room where everyone was waiting, her temper building with each step. Her cheeks were flushed, her head felt like it was going to split wide open, and she could feel every eye in the room on her.

She'd been blown totally away this morning when the realization dawned as to who the handsome man was who entered the conference room. Then coming face-to-face with Anthony had knocked her for a loop, he was still a gorgeous, sexy, tantalizing figure; even though he was a real ass. She pushed the conference room door open and barreled inside and resumed her seat between

Chase and Roberto, a torrent of emotions coursing through her fragile, tired and aching body.

CHAPTER NINE

"What the hell were you thinking, Ash?" Chase glared at his friend.

"Well Chase, I have been doing a lot of thinking in the past few days. It's kind of the nature of my job. You want to narrow it down a bit?"

"Ashley."

"You know how I feel about -----" She gritted her teeth, not wanting to think about Anthony and the tide of emotions their meeting had just jerked out of her. Damn. She didn't want to work with him. But he had said that Patrick was okay; maybe she could just go ahead and leave? No, then she would have to explain why she suddenly left and came home. She couldn't tell Uncle Morgan and Aunt Lynn anything yet. Damn and damn again.

Chase put his pen down and studied Ashley.

"You're lucky they didn't call the psychiatric ward and throw a straight jacket on you." Chase shook his head.

"So just throw me into the biggest, deepest, darkest pit you can find."

"I'll admit Anthony is a son of a bitch"

Ash's brow arched. "Worse!"

"Okay; worse than a son of a bitch. But you can't just run up and punch the man in the nose with a room full of cops, Ash." Chase finished.

Ash shook her head. "I don't know if I can do this, Chase." It was weird sitting there, looking across the room at Anthony who was still engrossed in conversation with the CIA Director. She ran her hands through her hair. She didn't want to admit the feelings that had ripped through her earlier. Every feeling she never wanted to experience again; and certainly not in response to Anthony.

"My advice to you is that you don't have a choice." Chase responded solemnly.

"What I need is another life and someone else to finish this one." Ashley grumbled.

"Ash, if you need anything, let Brenda or I know, but for now we have to remain focused; lives are at stake!"

"I know, I know. That is why I walked away before!" Ashley's voice lowered. Her eyes strayed to the front of the room where Tony was still in deep conversation with the director.

Chase clenched his teeth. "Whatever is going on between you two has to stay on the back burner until this operation is completed. We really have the chance to make a difference this time and get all the bad guys with one fatal swoop."

"Maybe, it is never that simple." Ashley signed. "I have seen too many well planned operations go to shit because of corrupt officials and dirty cops." Just a little jaded with justice right now."

Chase smiled ruefully. "This time we will take no prisoners and leave only their dead carcasses in our wake! Justice will prevail."

Anger clawed at her gut like a hungry animal and she bit her lip hard. "All right, I'm in one hundred percent, one last time."

"Good." Chase smiled, and then reached for one of the reports in the pile on the table. "Just keep your cool so we don't have to send the men in white coats after you!"

Ashley laughed. "But, crazy people don't know they're crazy!"

"Crazy people also don't question their own sanity." he said practically. "Jeez, sweetie, you're the sanest person I know."

"That doesn't say a lot for the company you keep." Ashley smirked with a roll of her eyes.

"Ditto." Chase threw his head back and laughed, then quickly sat up straight looking forward as Director Jones began to speak.

"We would like to apologize to each of you for the disruption earlier; a little unfinished personal business. Without any further delays, Agent Anthony Langston with the CIA will provide each of you with the specific details of the case thus far." Director Jones left Anthony at the podium in front of the room and took a seat at the front table.

"Thank you for being here today. I will cut straight to the chase. I have spent the past five years working my way up through the Martinelli Colombian Drug Cartel. I am currently the CEO for Adrianno Martinelli, under the assumed name of Victor Shayne. Adrianno has contracted four hits in the past six months. All four of these people are currently in the witness protection program; their future will be sorted out as soon as the operation is over. Adriano assumes they are dead, and that I killed them. I utilized bodies from morgues, and placed them in body bags for proof in some cases. Extensive facial wounds made the bodies virtually unrecognizable. I received information this morning that the largest drug shipment the states has ever seen will be arriving at midnight tomorrow night at the harbor behind the new Aztec Chemical Plant located in St. Andrews, Florida. The ships will come in and the parcels of pure cocaine and heroin will be offloaded into the plant warehouse. The Martinelli Cartel and his body guards will be on hand to cut the cocaine and repackage it for placement into specialized empty chemical containers. His men will randomly select packages and test for purity. The containers will then be loaded back onto the ships, planes and tractor trailers for disbursement to various locations. This abandoned airstrip is one that will be utilized by this operation. We currently have two CIA operatives on the inside working with us as well, so if anything changes we will know immediately. They have both been on the inside for a little over two years now. We will need to secure the port and arrest everyone there. This will have to be done with rapid speed to prohibit the alerts going out to disbursement locations. Our agents, including each of you will take over the ships, planes and trucks once the drugs have been loaded onto them and take them to their respective locations and facilitate a "sting operation" in order to secure the arrests of the future distributors on the other end. It will be one of the most costly, extravagant, intricate and complex undercover operations we have ever attempted and will require enormous manpower and exhaustive hours to accomplish. Folks this is our chance to finally make a difference. I will open the floor to any questions before I go into the specific details of the operation." Anthony leaned forward to the table beside the podium and lifted the pitcher of water to fill a small plastic cup. Little chips of ice slipped into the cup as the water flowed through the spout. He picked up the cup and downed it with one gulp.

"I have a question. How much firepower are we dealing with?" Roberto rummaged through the file on the table in front of Chase and Ashley.

"The most massive amounts of fully automatic weapons, and explosives you will ever see. So, full body armor will be a necessity." Anthony replied dryly.

"Is there something else you're not telling us?" Chase ground the question straight at Anthony.

"We will name this operation "sundown" and in answer to your question Chase, this will either be the most successful drug operation ever completed by dual law enforcement agencies or a full-fledged blood bath. Ricky Martinelli will be the captain of the lead ship of drugs coming into the port. We currently have six murder warrants for Ricky, and RICO Act Indictments. He was responsible for the explosion about five years ago that killed two agents, an eight member SWAT team and injured several others. We seized all assets related to Ricky at that time. Adrianno Martinelli sent his son Ricky into hiding and this will be his first trip back to the states. It is believed that Ricky has been in Costa Rico which does not honor extraditions. We will need all those warrants and indictments on hand as well." The militant look in Anthony's eyes indicated he was trying hard to control his emotions.

Ashley's head jerked up. That would be the explosion that almost killed her. It had also been the root of Anthony's demand that she quit the DEA. "Do you plan on having officers on the water as well as in the plant?" She glared at him.

He leaned against the podium and gripped the sides so tight that his knuckles appeared white. She was good; she still possessed that finely strung intuitive radar. More than once, she had picked up on something others missed and given them the key to solving a case in the past. Now, he couldn't imagine working with her. He knew not to cross her at this moment, maybe later. Right now his nose still sported the brunt of her last angry episode, and a part of him felt as if he deserved the punch. Damn, she was something.

"You bring up a most crucial point, Ms. Cameron." Anthony's gaze snagged Ashley's.

When she glanced up, his gaze captured hers and electricity raced through her body. That look could drag secrets out of her that she didn't want to own up to right now; even if he deserved to know.

She forced her eyes away from his, knowing the answer before she asked the next question. "And that would be?"

The vast amount of waterfront surrounding the back side of the warehouse creates an obstacle to be overcome. I have secured six shrimp boats for our agents to man, as they will not look conspicuous, we need more but, more would bring unwarranted attention. Explosive devices will need to be set in the water approximately fifteen hundred feet out from the shore. The timers on the explosives will need to allow for remote detonation. These will be utilized to keep the ships in port should they try to escape back out to sea with the drug cargo. Thus, the need for the navy seals team." Anthony gestured toward the six men seated at the third row of tables.

"These six men are the best demolition experts in the world."

"I hate to be the bearer of bad news, but there is a category four hurricane that is still building up strength in the gulf as we speak. Anticipated land fall is shortly after midnight tomorrow night. We need to make provisions to accommodate Mother Nature as St. Andrews was in the projected path last night." Chase informed the team in a slow, calm voice.

Anthony frowned. "Damn! How could we have missed that Jones?" He threw a portfolio down on the podium and glanced at his boss. "Jones, how could we have forgotten how volatile and unpredictable the weather is here in August?" This enlightening bit of information compromised the seal team, the pilots of the planes, choppers and the captains for the boats; not to mention the success of the whole operation.

Director Jones stood up from his seat. "Let's have the team take a fifteen minute break as it is obviously going to be a very long day. Chase, can you have your computer guy set up the downlink for the weather satellite in here right now? We need to get some coordinates on this thing and see where the projected landfall will be and what devastation is expected."

"Consider it done." Chase responded immediately to Director Jones request. "Greg go out to the car and pull all the computer equipment and bring it in here and set it up. Grayson and Roberto will help you." Chase commanded Greg by his real name this time, instead of referring to him like they usually did as "geek boy."

"Chase is there a soda machine around here?" Ashley was fumbling through her purse looking for change.

"Just down the corridor to the right." Chase pointed in the direction of the rear door to the conference room.

    Ashley found the soda machines, deposited four coins, pushed the button and patiently waited for the drink to fall in the slot below. She leaned down and picked up the drink while shifting the sliding strap of her heavy handbag back up on her shoulder. She went outside. The heat of the noon summers day hit her head-on. She fished through her suitcase of a purse looking for her sunshades, slid them gently on her face; and then quickly removed them as the pain seared through her head from their touch to her bruises. She leaned against the white block building in the shade of the roof's overhang and drew heavily on the cigarette she had just lit. Her red silk shirt was already beginning to cling to her skin from the intense humidity. Ashley looked down and saw the telltale signs of purplish-blue bruising on her upper and lower arms.

    Tears started forming in the corner of her eyes and she quickly brushed them away. Her whole life had been turned upside down this morning. She finished the cigarette and ground the butt out on the uneven pavement before leaning over and picking it up and tossing it in the garbage next to the door she had exited. She should be relieved. Patrick was alive and well. That was the sole purpose for her coming here anyway. It was a tremendous burden lifted to know he was safe. She had no desire to be part of an "Operation Sundown" but, she refused to quit anything until she saw it through to the end. Ashley popped the top on the soda can and tilted the can up to her red tinted lips. The cold liquid felt refreshing sliding down her throat. She stared at the light red stain her lips had left on the can. Anthony's appearance had opened up so many issues that she preferred to leave in the past. She had suffered too many shocks in the past forty-eight hours. So lost was she in her own thoughts that she didn't realize she had company until a shadow obscured the scorching light from the sun.

Ashley quickly glanced up as Anthony approached. He was here for an assignment and nothing more, shit. The past needed to stay just that - the past.

Her eyes looked over his tall lean frame with his clean cut appearance and piercing black eyes. "You look different than I remember."

He tugged at the tie around the neck of his shirt. "About two feet of hair gone; and I would still prefer to be dressed in a tank, shorts and flops."

"Of the latter I have no doubt." She finished the last of her soda and tossed the can in the garbage.

Damn if she wasn't gorgeous, he thought, standing there staring sternly at him with those sea-blue eyes. She'd pulled her hair back, but several dark strands had escaped and framed her porcelain looking face. He still wondered how she had acquired the nasty gash to her forehead and her arms were all bruised up and down. It certainly looked recent. The red sleeveless blouse she wore revealed long slender arms, arms that were now tucked under her breasts in a gesture of disapproval at his surveillance of her. As much as he wanted to continue admiring her more womanly attributes, he forced his attention to stay on her face.

"I came out here looking for you." Anthony began. He shifted his weight from one long leg to another.

"You came looking for me? Do you mean in the past five minutes or the past five years?" Ashley all but threw the words at him.

"We need to talk."

"No, we needed to talk over five years ago, before you walked out on me."

Anthony went still. "It wasn't like that Ash!"

"Now that is priceless; you were staying out drunk for nights at a time, weren't working and chasing skirts in the bar. And don't forget our first year together, I put up with your last ex-psycho girlfriend calling for a whole year, even sending naked pictures of herself to your phone, stalking every party we went too and not once did you ever tell her that you were in a relationship and not to call you anymore. I had to call a friend of mine that was a cop, to make her stop. You should have been man enough to have taken care of the problem to start with! I didn't blame her as much as I did you, because you led her on!" Ashley said through clenched teeth, choking back the tears.

"Ash, please, I refuse to play along with your

delusions."

"Don't call me that. As a matter of fact don't call me anything. Just go away. And delusions to you are reality to me! Go back to your rock-n-roll, biker, playboy lifestyle and leave me the hell alone!" She wasn't buying the sudden softness of his tone. Tony always had an agenda, an ulterior motive, and he wasn't above using false kindness, seductiveness, and dozens of bouquets of yellow roses to get his way. Well, for the first time since she had met him, she wasn't caving in and she saw him for what he really was, a coward!

"I can't accommodate you with going away." Anthony leaned forward.

Ashley backed away from him, but came up against the block wall of the building. She suddenly felt like a trapped animal. "What the hell do you want to talk about?"

"Us, I'm not leaving St. Andrews until we talk about everything that happened before. Give me a chance to explain." Anthony lowered his gaze.

"There is nothing left to discuss." Ashley tried to

keep all emotion out of her voice.

"Still not taking care of yourself?" Anthony gently brushed back a tendril of hair covering the nasty gash on her forehead.

She glared at him.

His expression was almost smug, as if he knew a secret that no one else did. But, she was the one with the secret. And a secret that she had no intention of revealing to him either. She was tempted not to answer, but decided against the idea. "I am taking care of myself just fine, thank you." She swallowed hard.

"Who hit you in the head?" He demanded.

"A Martinelli henchman. It happened early last night. He looks worse than I do; he's dead; if that is any consolation." Ashley grudgingly provided the requested information to Anthony. Knowing full well if she didn't, he could find out anyway.

"I would like a copy of the incident and autopsy report. You could bow out and go home now that you know Patrick is alive. I assume that is why you are here working, isn't it? I knew he was related to you somehow;

I just couldn't remember how." Anthony continued to study her face closely.

"I'm not leaving until I am good and ready, and thank you but no, once I start something, I always finish it. Unlike other people I know. Where is Patrick right now?" She questioned pointedly.

"You know I can't give you that information yet. I assure you he is safe. You will be the first one the information is provided to, at the appropriate time." He cleverly changed the subject. "Where are you living now?"

Ignoring the ache in her chest, which his gently question evoked, she set her jaw. "That is not related to the case and is absolutely none of your business." All color drained from her face, he was too close physically and closing in on her personal life as well. She felt like a small fish about to be devoured by a massive shark.

He stepped even closer. His gaze traveled over her creamy throat, luscious lips, and eyes the color of a stormy turquoise ocean, and her far too pale complexion. His fingers itched to touch her. "You are still a tantalizing temptation." His well-formed mouth lifted into a smile.

She couldn't quite hide the pain in her voice, "Likewise; but a temptation that I have no intention of succumbing to again." Ashley glanced around. There was no escape.

Despite her best attempts at blinking them back, a few tears trickled from the corner of her eyes. Damn him. What would it take for him to show her an ounce of decency, an iota of compassion, and just walk away? His hands caught hers and placed them on his shoulders. He slid his arms around her and pulled her tight against him. "What do you say Ash? Do you want to yield too, just for old time sake?"

"No." She whispered, just as his mouth closed down on hers. It was the most exotic kiss she could remember. Better than the first and the last time he had kissed her, she was losing her soul again; no she didn't have one, for Tony had taken it years ago. In the faint crevices of her mind she heard a little angel whisper….. "The past is lost in a sea of darkness forever and the future is but a faint glimpse on the horizon."

He lifted his head and gazed into her eyes. "You're still beautiful." His hands slipped beneath the flimsy red material of her shirt and covered her breasts. He didn't give her time to react and covered her mouth with his again. His fingers slid down her neck and the rest of her collarbone. His mouth followed his hand, nibbling.

She slid her hands from his shoulders to his chest, intending on pushing him away. But, her hands refused to move from his broad chest like they were fused there by pure heat. There wasn't an ounce of fat on the man.

He lifted his head and looked into her eyes once more, breathing heavily. "Do you want this, Ash?

She realized he was giving her a choice. Something he hadn't done five years ago. Anger and pent up emotions surfaced so quickly that before she could stop herself, she reached up and slapped him hard on the cheek.

"Since when does it matter to you, what I want? Ashley demanded. "You didn't give my feelings a second thought over five years ago and I'll be damned if you will start things back up where you left off. Go back to your psycho ex-girlfriend or your bar whores!" She swung away from his now loosened embrace and stomped off toward the door.

His grin spoke of mischief. "I have only just begun, sweetheart!" He devoured her sexy, retreating figure. He'd often fantasized about seeing her again; and much, much more. But this little piece of reality made his fantasies dim in comparison.

Ashley walked down the corridor to the elevators and viciously jabbed the button for the elevator to open. Chase was right; she did need to be in a straight jacket, just go ahead and call the men in the white jackets and have her committed. She hadn't raised a hand to anyone in anger for over five years now, and within a matter of hours she had struck out twice - both at an obnoxious, pig headed, arrogant man; Anthony Langston. The man simply made her totally and irrationally insane.

The doors to the elevator opened and she slid inside, quickly punching the second floor button. Silently praying that the doors would close quickly before anyone else got on, she had no desire for company at the moment. She bit her lip, still tasting the warmth of Anthony's lips. Needing something to stable her trembling legs, she grabbed the cool rail attached to the wall inside the elevator, and closed her eyes so as not to see her fractured reflection in the mirrored walls. Ashley felt a vague discomfort as she took on all the possibilities and discarded them just as quickly. She pushed aside her tumultuous thoughts. Everyone needed to concentrate on this case and conclude it, with no lives lost. Period! She didn't want anything more.

She had left all this drama behind and rebuilt her life. A.J. deserved a decent future. Ashley didn't feel she was cheating A.J. out of anything, not knowing a father that could just as easily have been a sperm donor for all the concern he had shown; wasn't denying him a damn thing.

But in her heart, she knew she wasn't admitting the truth.

CHAPTER TEN

It proved to be a long exhausting afternoon. The latest weather reports had the hurricane weakening some but barely missing St. Andrews, and Bay City Florida. They would still be on the receiving side of some very strong bands of winds, but plans were laid for "Operation Sundown" to proceed. They viewed an hour of slides consisting of blueprints of the entire chemical plant and warehouse. Definitive plans were made to reconvene at 10:00 a.m. again Friday morning, back at the conference room for any updates necessary. Anthony had left at approximately three-thirty p.m. for a pre-arranged meeting he had with Adrianno Martinelli. His piercing black eyes had sought her out of the crowded room. With an almost devilish smile he had mouthed "later," while sleekly and silently, slipping out the conference room door.

Shocked and angry with herself at the knowledge that she had felt any kind of attraction to Anthony after all this time. Ashley finally regained control of her frayed emotions and felt Chase staring at her.

"What?" She snapped.

"Are you okay?" Chase asked with a measure of concern.

"Fine." She lied and blinked, rapidly trying to regain her defenses. "Did you know Anthony was going to be here?"

Chase sighed. "Ashley, my brain hasn't been completely fried by the tropical sun. I would have told you, had I known. No one has seen Anthony since he left here a little over five years ago."

Anger pulsed off in her. "What I really want is for him to disappear again and to be left the hell alone. He just reappears and expects to pick up where we left off."

Chase's brow arched. "A little late for that, I'm afraid. You know he will learn the truth about A. J., sooner or later."

Ashley folded her arms tight against her chest. "Like hell he will." She refused to acknowledge the ugly realization of where things were headed.

"Well, punching him in the nose the first time you see him in five years has to make him wonder at the intensity of your response." Chase reasoned.

She hung her head slightly. "That's not all; I slapped him in the parking lot earlier too!"

"I don't want to know why!" Chase shook his head. "I called Brenda earlier and she is going to meet us for dinner at *Bays Steak House*."

Although Ashley might appear to be handling the situation well, Chase saw the telltale signs of her tension by the way she was now tapping her fingernails rhythmically on the table.

Everyone was vacating the parking lot like NASCAR drivers finishing their final lap. Right before she and Chase reached the Jag; the tall, thin, bald headed man with the John Lennon glasses pulled up beside them in a black Z-71 Tahoe.

"You're Ashley Cameron, aren't you?" The man extended his hand out the window to flip the ash from his cigar.

"Yes, sir." Ashley answered, unsure of the identity of this man.

Chase walked around the Jag to where Ashley was standing. "Ashley this is Mr. Lawrence, he is the Director of the FBI. We haven't seen you around much lately, Mr. Lawrence?"

"No Chase, I have been on a trip abroad for a while, burning some vacation time. I don't think Ashley here, remembers me?"

"No sir, I can't place you." Ashley frowned slightly, trying to remember this man.

"It was about twelve years ago, an operation you worked crossed state lines over into New Orleans. It doesn't matter; glad to have you aboard on this one. You know Anthony, don't you?" Mr. Lawrence questioned.

"Mr. FBI, I don't mean to be disrespectful, but my personal life is of no concern to this operation. You have a real good evening." With that Ashley turned on her heel and approached the passenger side of the Jag, patiently waiting for Chase to unlock the door. She could barely discern whatever Chase mumbled to Mr. Lawrence before joining her at the car.

Chase got in shaking his head. "Damn, Ash; just slam the FBI Director, why don't you!"

Three minutes after they were seated at Bays Steak House, the drinks they ordered arrived. Ashley was still staring, stunned, out the stained glass windows of the restaurant; pondering what was motivating Anthony to infiltrate the drug cartel. To literally give up five years of his life, he had to be driven by something or someone. She wondered if there was someone in his life. Was he married? Had more children? More children......that would mean that A. J., would have half-brothers or sisters somewhere. She just wanted to go back to the life she had in D.C., with no upsetting changes to explain to A. J. She glanced down at the gin and tonic she'd ordered and then lifted a speculative gaze to Brenda and Chase, her face drained of color.

Brenda glanced at Ashley. "I'm sorry–"

She shook her head. "It will be okay." But from her body posture, her shoulders hunched as if to protect her, it wasn't. Taking a deep breath, she hid her emotions behind that cool detective mask of hers. It was one of the few things that she still had control over. Finally, she shook her head and leaned back in her chair. "Well this is just too perfect an ending for today." She replied sarcastically, waving to the waitress for another round.

Before Brenda or Chase could respond, the waitress returned with more drinks for all three of them.

Chase downed his bourbon and coke. "I understand. It's been one of those days Ashley, but you have to get a grip or pull out of the investigation. Tomorrow night is going to be the devil of an operation to pull off. Are you sure you are up to handling that right now?"

"I have to." Ashley quickly answered.

"Okay, we will help you deal with your demons later. You know that A. J. is doing fine with your aunt and uncle and that Anthony knows nothing about A. J., so he is not a threat to either of you at this time. Anthony told me earlier when you stepped out of the meeting that Patrick was okay. He also said that he had only told you and I and that we could not tell anyone yet.

Right now you have to concentrate on the operation. I don't want to see you or any of the other cops killed. You know what Martinelli is capable of doing." Chase's eyes hardened, remembering the blood bath of over five years ago.

Brenda took a sip of her red wine. "I can only imagine how shocked you were this morning, to see Anthony again after all these years. But, Chase is right. Why don't you let the guys handle the operation now that you know that Patrick is okay?"

"I just can't." She ran her fingers through her long dark hair. "I started this investigation, now I have to see it through to the end. Besides, I want to know for sure that Patrick is alright." Ashley twirled the ice around in her gin and tonic with the small slender red straw provided.

"Oh, come on, Ash." Doubt and disbelief rang in his words. "I know that Anthony is an inconsiderate ass but, he wouldn't lie about Patrick's safety."

"I know that. I just know that Martinelli is capable of anything. He just tried to have me taken out.

And, that is something that has really been bothering me. Anthony knew nothing of the attempted hit on my life last night; he told me that he would get a copy of the incident report. He is supposed to be the top man right now in the Martinelli Cartel. Anthony may only know what Martinelli wants him to know, or there is a setup about to go down. Until we have both Adrianno and Ricky Martinelli in custody, Patrick really isn't safe." She cocked her head. "As a matter of fact, none of us are."

"I was wondering about that myself. Martinelli is a very shrewd business man, however illegal his businesses may be. For him to turn total control over to Anthony, or should I say Victor Shayne his assumed identification; would certainly take a lot of compromising on Anthony's part. Martinelli would have made Anthony commit unspeakable illegal acts to prove his allegiance to the cartel. I know it has been a little over five years, but I am just not convinced that Anthony is in as deep as he thinks, either." Chase was solemn faced.

Before they could say anything more, their steaks and fries arrived. Ashley ordered another round of drinks and busied herself pouring mustard on her fries.

Brenda took a bite of her salad. "What did you say to Anthony this morning?"

Chase laughed. "Before or after she punched him in the nose and slapped him in the face?" His humor punched a hole in the tense atmosphere.

"You didn't?" A responding laugh bubbled up in Brenda.

Ashley grabbed a fry, dipped it in mustard and popped it into her mouth. "Yes, I did. I suppose I went a little psycho. I mean all the pent up emotions of not knowing if Anthony was dead or alive for so long - I wanted to kill him and at the same time, I was relieved that he was alive. There always existed a fine line between love and hate for us."

Snorts of laughter erupted from Brenda and Chase.

"Do you still love him?" Brenda compassionately asked.

"I do still love him but, I will never allow him back in my life to hurt me or A. J. again. I could never trust that he wouldn't just decide to disappear off the face of the earth again. That would not be fair to A. J." Ashley managed a smile attempting to hide the pain in her heart.

Brenda saw through her best friend's futile attempt. "Is it possible that Anthony has changed?"

"My dad once told me a story about a little girl that was walking through the woods and came across a rattlesnake. It was the dead cold of winter and the snake begged the little girl to pick him up and place him under the warmth of her jacket. The little girl refused at first, stating that he was a snake and that he would bite her. The snake continued to beg until the little girl gave in and picked him up and placed him under the warmth of her jacket. The snake warmed his body then struck out and bit the little girl. The little girl cried, why did you bite me - you promised that you would not. The snake replied - you knew I was a snake when you picked me up!" Ashley downed her third gin and tonic; alcohol, in sufficient quantities, is Novocain for the brain. The trouble is that when it wears off, all the pain and memories are still there, plus a headache.

"So in answer to your question, I have no intention of going there again. I know he is still a snake and I have already had enough of his poison to last me a lifetime. He gave me one wonderful blessed gift in A. J. You see, the best thing he ever did in his entire life, he knows nothing about!." Ashley finished, avoiding their faces.

"So you've decided to pursue your investigation through to the closure of "Operation Sundown," unless hell freezes over." Chase took another bite of his steak, deciding a change of subject was in order.

She sighed. "I'm right, and you know it."

"Apparently, hell just froze," Brenda knowingly smiled as she took another bite of her salad.

"And hell hath no fury........."

Chase was cut off from finishing his sentence by Brenda's sharp elbow to his ribs.

Ashley mentally scolded herself. What she needed was some time and distance away from everyone, some time alone to clear her head for the operation tomorrow night. "Chase does DEA still have men assigned to the beach house detail?"

Chase massaged the back of his neck. "Yes. Why?"

"I just need some time alone to think and clear my head before the operation tomorrow night. I would like to go out to the beach house, if Trent won't mind?" Ashley braced herself, ready for Chase to adamantly refuse.

"We still have two men on the detail. Trent won't care, but; I don't think it is a good idea for you to go back out there."

"I will be fine, Chase. I just really need some time alone. You can take me out there and make sure everything is okay."

"I suppose I can drive you out there and check the place out good." Chase glanced at the dial of his Rolex. "It is already 7:00 pm; we are going to catch some of Craig's game. We need to go ahead and go as I have to come back to the office and pick up some paperwork for the meeting in the morning, before going to the game."

"I can drive Trent's jeep back to yours and Brenda's house in the morning. That will save some time." Ashley grabbed her bag as the trio got up to leave the restaurant.

"Chase, why don't you go ahead and go by the office and pick up what you need for the morning meeting, since you are closer to your office from here. Ashley can go ahead and go home with me and collect what she needs from our house and be ready when you get there. You can meet me at the game after you drop Ash off." Brenda leaned over the table to secure her bag from underneath.

Chase planted a quick kiss on Brenda's lips. "Thanks, babe. I am glad one of us is thinking logically. I am just too tired to think straight tonight. I'll see you girls at home shortly."

Brenda pulled the car out of the parking lot of Bays Steakhouse. Dark shadows danced around the car as the restaurant sat off the road with a dimly lit parking lot.

"You're wrong, Ashley." Brenda stated softly.

"About what?" she snapped.

"Not telling Anthony the truth about A. J. I can understand your wanting to wait until this operation is over, and I think you should. But, you do need to tell him the truth. Regardless of how things ended between you two over five years ago, he is still A. J.'s father. And, you said A. J. had begun to ask questions. Those questions are not going to get any easier for you to answer." Brenda smiled sympathetically at Ashley.

"But, what if I tell him and he wants to meet A. J., and then just disappears out of his life? Ashley murmured.

"What if you don't allow him that chance and A. J. grows up thinking you deliberately kept him from his father? Are you prepared to deal with that?" Brenda turned down the residential street to their house.

"I know your right; it is just so much to think about. That is really why I wanted to be alone tonight. I hope you understand."

Brenda pulled into their carport, switched the car off and reached over and squeezed her best friend's hand.

"Of course I understand. Just think through everything carefully. I think you still love Anthony. I don't think you have ever allowed yourself to get over him. When Anthony just up and left, I'm sure it left many unanswered questions. Maybe this time you will find some resolution, one way or another."

"Thanks Brenda."

"I'll help you collect what you need from here. Just promise you will call me when you get settled in for the night at the beach house?

"I will." Ashley crossed her heart in a solemn promise.

The duo went upstairs and began to collect Ashley's belongings. Brenda carefully folded while Ashley simply slung clothes into her bag. They descended the stairs just as Chase entered the door.

"Are you sure you want to go back out to the beach house?" Chase dropped his briefcase and files on the foyer table.

"Yes, Chase, I am certain. I just really need some time alone to think. I will be fine."

"Okay. I know it would be pointless to argue with you. The guys are still pulling surveillance on the place, so it should be safe enough."

Ashley walked past him with Brenda in tow, taking her bags out to the Jaguar.

"You might need these." Chase tossed the keys to Brenda.

"Thanks." His wife gave him a knowing smile. They were both extremely worried about the wisdom of Ashley's decision but, they both knew when she set her mind to do something……"

Soon, Ashley was kissing Brenda on the cheek and promising again to call when she settled in at the beach house. The drive to the beach passed quickly and in total silence.

Chase talked to the officers briefly before they entered the cottage. He promptly checked all the windows and patio doors to make sure they were all secure, before collecting Ashley's bags from the trunk and carrying everything upstairs and dropping them in a heap on her bed.

There was an awkward moment of silence. Thunder cracked and rolled in the distance.

"I need to leave in order to make it back to see part of the game before the rain from the hurricane starts approaching and it gets called." Chase gave Ashley a quick embrace and left her to her own devices. "Don't forget to call Brenda." He called back over his shoulder.

"I will." Ashley watched through the double pane glass windows as lightning flashed again and again, casting an eerie orange glow over the white wicker furniture inside the beach cottage. The whitecaps in the ocean were lit up by the sharp streaks of lighting jumping across the ocean's surface.

Ashley shivered. She had never felt so all alone in her life, so profoundly confused and so cold on the inside. It was like a part of her was dead and there was no way to resurrect the dead.

She walked away from the windows and placed her purse on top of the bar in the kitchen. She reached down and plucked her cell phone from the purse confines. Quickly she dialed Brenda's number before she forgot to make good of her earlier promise, as she sank thankfully into the ocean printed oversized cushions of the king size wicker sofa. Moments later she clicked the phone closed and continued staring out the windows. She was still sitting there staring out the window thirty minutes later as the palms started bending beneath the strain of the winds. Rain pelted against the window panes.

    The agents were in two cars outside, one positioned at each corner of the cottage. They took turns getting out of their cruisers to do walk around checks of the entire perimeter of the cottage. Ashley checked her cell for messages and returned a call to her Chief Investigator Larry regarding an on-going investigation he was having some problems with in D.C. She made another quick phone call to A. J. before ascending the stairs to run a warm luxurious bubble bath.

    An hour later she was basking in the warmth of the lavender scented white puffy bubbles. The water was so hot it had steamed over all the mirrors in the garden oasis bathroom. Classical music floated around her, soothing her body and mind. Ashley closed her eyes, silently clearing her mind and reveling in the experience of total relaxation. Sudden memories, ones she had wanted to erase kept flashing before her like scenes from an old movie. A movie whose final scene was ingrained in her heart forever and never changed.

Heart of Jaded Justice

CHAPTER ELEVEN

"Are you trying to drown yourself?" Anthony's dark silky like voice drawled from the arched doorway to the garden oasis.

Ashley's eyes snapped open and she bolted upright from the massive bubble filled tub, slipped clumsily against the ceramic bottom and slid completely underwater.

She came up sputtering, "What the hell are you doing here?" How did you get in here?" She stammered angrily, coughing water from her lungs.

The militant look in Ashley's eyes told Anthony that she was fighting her temper. He knew not to cross her at this moment. He stopped inches from the huge Jacuzzi tub and extended his hand, holding a lush mint green and white bath towel just within her reach.

"Are you going to answer me?" She shouted at Anthony, while snatching the towel from his hand, stepping out of the water and quickly covering her white foam covered body with the towel. Heat raced over her skin at his scorching stare. He made her feel as if she had no towel covering her body.

"Which question should I answer first?" Anthony smirked.

"Just get out, now." Ashley pointed at the door almost losing the grip she had on her towel.

"I need to talk to you Ash." Anthony continued to stare at her gorgeous towel clad body, admiring the way the bubbles were dissolving away to reveal even more creamy colored flesh.

"Don't you know how to use a damn phone? But, no that would be too civilized for you wouldn't it? You prefer to make as grand of an entrance as you do an exit." Ashley wanted to strangle him; instead she threw the glass bottle of lavender bath salts at his head.

"Now, now; there is no need for violence." Anthony's panther like reflexes caught the glass container with ease.

He had on tight fitting jeans and a black button

up shirt with the sleeves rolled up. Her gaze caught the trickling of dark hair covering the tan expanse of his broad chest revealed beneath the unfastened buttons of his shirt.

"You still ask the questions and answer them for yourself, without giving anyone a chance to answer." Anthony stepped closer; his chest was inches from her face.

Her gaze traveled up his throat to his chin then his wonderful sensuous lips. Her fingers itched to touch him. "Maybe that is because I would be waiting for hell to freeze over to get an honest answer from you!"

His well-formed mouth lifted into a smile. She felt his eyes move over her body, silently stripping her of all covering. "You are still an earth moving temptation."

Her gaze locked with his.

"A temptation that I need to surrender to!" He caught her hands in his and the fluffy white towel slowly slid to the floor. He slid his arms around her, pulling her against him. "What do you say Ash? Do you want this, too?"

She opened her mouth to say something obscene but, nothing came out. His soft mouth silently closed over hers in a soul wrenching kiss. Her turquoise eyes were suddenly very brilliant.

"God, Ashley, I want you. Right now I feel as if I have to have you to chase your demons from my dreams."

"My demons?" she taunted.

He bent down abruptly and scooped her into his arms, his expression taunt and hard with desire. "Yes, yes, your demons. You've been driving me crazy for five long years. I no sooner arrive back here in Florida than you show up."

As he spoke he was carrying her through the archway and out into the bedroom. He sat down with her on the bed, letting her rest across his thighs to lie cradled in his arms. Anthony stared down at her as she nestled against him. He was aware of the high level of his own frustration and knew that it wasn't merely physical in nature.

The frustration he was experiencing tonight

wasn't going to be extinguished by making Ashley his again. What he felt was a far more serious form of dissatisfaction. And it was born out of primal fear. Once he and Ashley had accomplished their investigation here in Bay City, there was nothing to keep her with him, and Anthony wanted to lash out violently against that knowledge. He had nothing to offer her to induce her to stay, and he knew it. He wanted to stay here in Bay City, but not without her. Anthony didn't even know how Ashley had rebuilt her life or whom she might have rebuilt it with. It drove him insane thinking of her in the arms of another man. Contemplating a future with her was very much a fantasy at this point. However, a fantasy that had kept him alive for years.

Almost as if against her own will, her hands trembled as she began undressing him. Willingly she let the passion of the moment push the unsettling, hopeless thoughts out of her mind. There was no point thinking about tomorrow. Hadn't she learned that lesson a long time ago?

He could feel her fingertips toying with the

buttons of his shirt. Her touch made him groan, and the evidence of his desire seemed to encourage her. She had his shirt off shortly and tossed to the floor. He felt the faint sting of her nails as they circled his flat, male nipples and tugged sensuously at the hair of his chest. Her mouth began to wander across the bare skin of his shoulder, and he felt a sharp tremor as she used her teeth to nip enticingly.

Anthony groaned as the delicate curve of her breast filled his palm, and he grazed the budding nipple lightly, fiercely excited when it began to harden beneath his touch. When the tip of each breast had hardened to his satisfaction, Anthony settled her back against the bed, sprawling aggressively on top of her. Then he lowered his head to taste the buds he had molded.

The lavender scent of her invaded his senses as he sucked at each nipple. He would never forget the fragrance of her, Anthony thought disturbingly. It would be imprinted on him for the rest of his life. That thought made him long to leave her with a memory of himself that she would never be able to escape.

"I want you to think of me when you go home, wherever that is now." he heard himself rasp. "I want you to see me, feel me, be aware of me every time you look at another man. I want to be in the way every time you think of going to bed with someone else!"

"You're so cruel Anthony. Don't you know you already have been?" Ashley whispered.

"I know, I'm cruel. With you I can't seem to help it. You do something to me, sweetheart, bring out the part of me that's been safely buried for such a long, long time." He slid down along her body, raining hot, damp kisses on her stomach. Then he plunged his fingers into the moist silky wetness between her thighs. Anthony knew even as he did it, this wasn't the way he had envisioned making love to her again after so many years. He had wanted to make it romantic and civilized, with all the nuances she would remember as sophisticated and exciting.

But he couldn't shake the sense of desperation that drove him, the almost violent desire to force himself on her. The thought that he could be losing her soon impelled him tonight as he made love to her atop the ornate flowered comforter of the bed.

She didn't resist him, didn't try to slow him or ask him to go more gently. Her willing acceptance of his mastery increased his restless desire even as it fed his satisfaction. She seemed to be as caught up in the urgent, primitive passion as he was, and that knowledge made his head reel.

Anthony moved his hands to tighten them around the rounded flesh of her buttocks, and Anthony caught his breath as his blood raced. He heard the soft moan at the back of her throat as he buried his lips in the hollow of her shoulder.

Then she was shakily undoing the fastening of his jeans and he drew himself slightly away so that she could finish undressing him.

"Ashley, Ashley, I want you so!"

"Yes, Anthony. Oh, yes!"

He kicked off his jeans and then came back down on her, hungrily parting her thighs so that he could indulge himself fully in the heat of her. When her fingers grasped roughly in his hair, Anthony glowed in the knowledge that he could make this one woman come so beautifully, excitingly alive. The way she surrendered to his touch was unlike anything he had ever known, it was like magic.

With infinite enjoyment he probed the secrets of her body, searching out the most sensitive places and teasing the welcoming flesh until Ashley was writhing and twisting beneath him.

He momentarily raised his head to stare at her. Her beautiful eyes were shut tightly and her lips were parted and moist as she panted in her excitement. She moaned softly, arching her hips into his hand, pleading with his body for the satisfaction it promised.

Totally enthralled, Anthony placed his hand to the damp, throbbing heart of her desire and marveled at the heat of her.

"You're on fire for me, honey. Molten lava fire. Open your eyes so I can drown in their stormy depths."

"Come to me, Anthony." she whispered hoarsely, pulling at his shoulders. "Come close to me. Please, she begged, eyes wide open."

As he slid slowly up to take what she offered, Anthony felt her soft, tender hands move down his waist. When she captured his manhood in her fingers, he growled his need, whispering short, blunt words of encouragement in her ear. "Good, girl. Good, girl."

Her hands teased him, just as he had been teasing her, promising everything with reckless abandon.

"Guide me" he ordered huskily. "Put me inside you, honey. Show me where you want me to go."

Instead of doing as he commanded, however, Ashley held him in exquisite captivity. Her palm cupped him and her fingers explored with gentle excitement, over and over again.

"Ashley!"

Still she teased and provoked and taunted. Her legs shifted alongside his, making him fully aware of the satin softness next to his own hair-roughened thigh. She continued brushing her moist silkiness up and down his thigh. "Sweetheart, you can't keep me out in the cold any longer." he vowed.

He thrust himself, plunging deeply into the dark velvet warmth of her waiting womanhood.

Beneath him Ashley gasped as she always had when he made her his. He felt her body accommodating him, closing around him, and in that moment Anthony experienced again the overwhelming urge to give her a child. His child. He let the fantasy take hold, just as he had let it take hold the other times he had made love to her. He longed to satisfy her as a woman, to make it possible for her to experience the physical pleasure of lovemaking. But on a deeper level he wanted so much more. He wanted to know that he had left a fertile seed in her as a talisman against the future. He knew if they had a child, she would never leave him. He had often thought and regretted over the years that they never had a child, maybe if they had - they would never have had to part, she would have given up her career, and he wouldn't have felt the need to go to the lengths he had to ensure her safety when Martinelli had taken out a very high dollar contract on her.

But his fantasy was not a civilized one. It was not

a jaded thing but, in turn extended their lovemaking.

With Ashley beneath him and the fantasy in his head, everything seemed to explode for Anthony in a white hot heat. He took his woman in a storm of need and desire, exulting in her equally explosive response. When he felt the delicious tremors take hold, rippling through her, he knew she had found her own satisfaction. That knowledge unloosed his own satisfaction.

Arching heavily against her, Anthony gave himself up to the pulsating release, crying out Ashley's name in an agony of fulfillment as he collapsed against her breasts.

It was a long time before either of them stirred. Ashley stirred, aware of the masculine weight that was still crushing her into the softness of the bed. Slowly her lashes lifted and a soft tender smile played at the corner of her mouth as she met Anthony's eyes and lifted one of his hands. "Beautiful," she murmured, stroking her fingers across the top of his tanned strong hand. "Your hands," she whispered, placing her lips to the palm of his hand. "You have the most beautiful hands in the whole world. I've never seen anything quite like them."

He smiled reluctantly, forcing himself to adopt a bantering tone. "The better to feel you with, my dear!"

"If you're going to adopt that attitude, I'd better not go on listing your best attributes," she complained. "It could go to your head."

"Don't stop now, please."

"Fishing for compliments? she teased, relishing in the aftermath of their passion. So afraid that this special moment would not last long, and she wanted to store up all the tenderness and the memories she possibly could. They were unique and they would remain so for the rest of her life. Ashley knew that beyond a shadow of doubt. They had forged more bonds than Anthony even knew about. She would never forget him. But then, she'd spent years realizing and fighting this very sentiment.

"I'll return your compliment with a compliment. I will tell you that you have the most beautiful eyes I have ever seen. A man can lose his soul in their depths. They are the color of a calm sea when you are happy and cheerful; the color of the sea after a storm when you are angry, excited or aroused." Anthony traced the edges of her eyelids with soft gentle fingertips, touched her mouth with his own in a slow, satisfied kiss.

All at once, Anthony jumped up and slapped Ashley playfully on her bare buttocks. "Up and at em, woman. I've performed my manly functions and put you promptly in your place. Now feed me, I'm starving."

"Typical male, all you ever think about is food and sex." she pouted.

"No, my dear. You have that one wrong. It is sex and then food!" He lunged, grabbing her lightly around her tiny waist and tossing her over his shoulder. "First, let's shower, lady. Then you can fix me something to eat."

The fantasy world they had created in the aftermath of their lovemaking; being two happy lovers without a care in the world or a future to consider, persisted right through breakfast. Ashley was strongly aware that she was deliberately trying to prolong it, and it seemed that Anthony was just as eager to go along with the illusion.

She was sitting across from Anthony at the

kitchenette bar staring at the strong features of his face, thinking how much A. J. looked like his father.

"What's wrong?" Anthony asked instantly, seeing the line of her brows furrow.

Ashley hesitated inhaling deeply as she glanced up at the clock on the wall. "It is 9:00 am and we have to be at the conference room for final debriefing at 10:00 am this morning."

"Surely you're not planning on seeing this operation through now? There really is no need for you to continue. I want you to quit, now, do you hear me?" Anthony reflectively agonized over the incident years ago when he demanded that she quit the DEA.

"Yes I hear you."

"Well are you going to quit?" Anthony demanded.

"I most certainly am not going to quit the operation. I gave my word that I would see it through to the end, and unlike some people I know........my word means something to me. I am going upstairs to finish getting dressed and I strongly suggest you do the same".

She glanced at his bare chest above his jeans and shoes. She had to concentrate; she simply would not allow him to distract her; this close to ending the operation. She had made a promise to the Director for DEA when she accepted the temporary assignment and she would be damned if Anthony would disrupt her plans. He had definitely caused enough disruption in her life already.

"I will drive myself to the meeting as I have to meet Chase at his house first." Ashley glared at Anthony before crossing to the sink and tossing the remains of her coffee down the drain.

"Ashley, we seriously need to talk about us before tonight." Anthony spoke softly as if the words were drug from his soul. She silently rinsed the cup before placing it in the dishwasher, ignoring his request for them to talk before leaving. Anthony solemnly stared at Ashley as she stomped up the staircase leaving him behind. Her dark hair swung behind her like a cloak, stopping just above the tight jeans covering her perfectly rounded derriere.

"We will talk later, Ashley." Anthony called up the staircase as he reached over to the sofa and pulled his shirt on.

Ashley watched from the upstairs window as Anthony saluted the two agents on duty outside before climbing into his vehicle and speeding down the drive. "Damn him to hell and back. How dare he think he could just waltz back into my life and make such demands?" Ashley muttered to herself.

CHAPTER TWELVE

Moments later Ashley had locked up and was climbing into the jeep. She glanced at her watch and cursed under her breath. She was going to be late. She sped down the driveway, entered the numbers on the keypad and waited patiently as the gate opened.

"How did Anthony get in last night?" Ashley murmured to herself as she sped down the road. He undoubtedly knew the password or had connections with the two agents providing surveillance on the cottage. She rummaged through her purse and pulled out her cell phone, quickly dialing Chase's number.

"Where are you?" barked Chase after only one ring.

"I am running late. I just called to tell you that I would meet you out at the airport conference room. There is no need for both of us to be late."

"Damn, Ashley. I told you to stay with Brenda and I. Well, just hurry up. I will let everyone know that you are on your way. Hey, you sound strange, are you okay?"

"No, but I will be. I will tell you and Brenda all about it later. We have more important things to worry about now." Ashley knew she was lying, she really wasn't okay.

"We'll fix whatever the problem is, don't worry. See you in a few." Chase abruptly ended the call.

Ashley held the silent receiver to her ear for a few seconds before clicking the phone closed and securing it in its clip to her belt. This way she wouldn't have to fish it out of her handbag again later. "What was she going to do? She still loved Anthony but, it simply could not be. She couldn't take another chance on him; the last time had left her almost destroyed. She would tell him about A. J., eventually. She felt that was the only right thing to do. Anthony would never have time for A. J. anyway. He would simply go back to whatever life he had been living before, whatever it was that was so important that he walked out on her the first time. Probably a long line of one-night stands and plenty of expensive liquor. It had literally driven her crazy over the years thinking of him in the arms of another woman, much less several other women.

She glanced out the window at the coastline, looking out on the horizon where the blue-green of the ocean usually met the clear blue of the sky. This morning the horizon was obliterated by massive dark storm clouds. The rain had subsided if only momentarily as the hurricane had the surf kicked up much higher than normal. A. J. would love it out here, rain or shine. Once the operation was over and Anthony had left town, she would fly A. J. down for a nice long vacation. She maneuvered the dirt lane at the old rusty sign pointing toward the County Line Airport. She crossed behind the iron fencing to the parking garage in the rear. Finding Chase's Jaguar, she slid the Jeep into the corresponding parking place; quickly grabbing her briefcase as she locked and exited the vehicle. Her stomach was churning as she jabbed the elevator button and tapped her boots repeatedly on the tile waiting for the doors to slide open. Ashley followed the corridor to the doors to the conference room and quietly pushed the rear door open. Glancing across the room she located Chase and headed to the seat beside him.

"We've been missing you, Ms. Cameron. So glad you could take the time out of your busy schedule to join us in a timely manner. Would you like to share with the group as to the reason for your tardiness?" Anthony's silky voice drawled from the podium in the front of the conference room, as his eyes found and locked with hers.

His choice of words was pointedly deliberate and she quickly digested them, tearing her gaze from his and dropping it to the glass of water which Chase was passing to her. He obviously felt no sympathy whatsoever for her tension and proceeded ahead without giving her the opportunity to say a word.

"It is 10:30 a.m. ladies and gentlemen and we have a lot of ground to cover before tonight. I have a four o'clock meeting with Adrianno Martinelli and his son Ricky should be present as well. I may not be able to meet with any of you again until "Operation Sundown" is off the ground and running tonight." Anthony handed Director Jones a stack of folders to distribute to everyone.

"You will find your assignments defined in the folders being given out. Please review your positions and the time frames carefully. There is no room for error. Chase will be the major point of contact during my absence. Ashley, Grayson and Roberto will be heading up the land assignments. Greg will be monitoring all radio communications. The Navy Seal Team will handle taking over the shipments coming in - this needs to be accomplished prior to these ships reaching the port at the warehouse, remember to set up the explosive about fifteen hundred feet out with remote detonation capability in the event the ships try to escape. We already have six shrimp boats out in the water manned by agents at this time. Keep in mind there are twenty three ships coming in from 9:00 pm until 12:00 pm. We don't need any choppers in the air until after midnight. Both Adrianno and Ricky Martinelli will be inside with me, along with two other CIA Agents presently working undercover at the plant. We will arrive at the port at some point as the ships arrive; they always check several ships at random when they arrive. They will cut a few of the bags of drugs and test them for purity before they are offloaded to be placed in the drum containers. Once the testing is completed, we will have secured the chain of custody to Adrianno and Ricky Martinelli and the arrests will take place. Remember the vast number of men in the Martinelli Cartel with each of them packing fully automatic weapons as well as hand grenades. ATF Agents will be canvassing the whole parking/perimeter of the plant. Every Operative involved has a picture in the packets you are receiving. Review these closely - it is essential that you know who the enemy is and that you don't fire on one of your own. Remember once we have secured all arrests at the Port, the ships must be loaded with the cargo and immediately be in route to their designated locations. This way we conduct a "sting" operation and arrest the buyers as well." Anthony stepped from the podium to pick up one of the paper cups and fill it with water. He downed the cup in one swallow as he glanced around assessing the room.

"I will attempt to answer any questions you may have now?"

"I am sure it is in the literature but, I assume you will be wired?" Chase asked.

"Yes, I will be wired, transmission will be video and audio. I will say, It is way past sundown on the horizon." At this time everyone will move quickly in unison. Timing is essential. The ships have to remain secured as the remaining agents flood the area and attach themselves to the Cartel. The Cartel will be alongside me, the CIA agents, and the Martinelli's. I want Chase, Grayson and Roberto to move in to assist in securing the Martinelli's. Ashley will remain behind to assist Greg in monitoring the radio traffic as it will become chaotic at this time. The ground units of the Alcohol, Tobacco and Firearms guys and the SWAT Team will approach from the east and the Drug Enforcement and FBI guys will enter from the west.

Ashley shook her head, taking offense to his

dismissal of her in securing the arrest of the Martinelli's. She stared at him, through him, her eyes becoming unfocused. He still refused to acknowledge her abilities and treat her as an equal member of this taskforce. No different than six years earlier.

Anthony was watching her, trying to read Ashley's expressions. Was he overreacting......trying too hard to protect her?

If he put himself out to be charming instead of challenging, would it make any difference? He just couldn't risk it; too many lives were at stake. Not to mention the woman he was in love with......

"How about we all take a quick break for about fifteen minutes? Let's meet back in here by one-fifteen pm." Anthony turned away from everyone and became deeply engrossed in a conversation with Director Jones.

She sighed. Her eyes reflected a wariness of spirit that Chase picked up on immediately.

"You must be about ready to burn one?" Chase said in an attempt to get her to smile as they exited through the back door.

"I sure am." Ashley reached in her purse and pulled out her cigarettes and lighter. She lit the end and inhaled strongly.

"What are you thinking?" Chase asked.

"I'm just not sure this is going to work. There are so many people involved. I'm afraid someone will get hurt or worse........

"Stop, Ashley." Chase interrupted. "It is more than the operation, admit it."

She wished to God she was most people, wished that her heart could understand what her brain did, that Anthony would be leaving soon, that she would probably never see him again. She wished to God that it didn't matter nearly as much as it did.

And if wishes were horses, her father used to say, we'd all ride away.

"Anthony came to the cottage last night." Ashley looked down at the smoke spiraling from the end of her cigarette.

"Did you guys talk?" Chase asked.

"Not exactly." She flushed and couldn't hold his

gaze, dropping her cigarette, grinding it under her shoe then picking it up and placing it in the can beside the wall.

He lifted a brow. "Well, you have to tell him how you feel and about A. J."

"I know, I know. I was soaking in a bubble bath when he just appeared in the doorway. I was so startled that I almost drowned myself. One thing led to another and we talked very little. Then this morning we were beginning to talk when Anthony became angry because I intended to finish the "Sundown Operation." I stomped upstairs and told him I would drive myself to the meeting." she said with exasperation.

"Ashley," he said quietly. "You can talk to Anthony tonight after the operation is over. I have seen the way he looks at you, I know he still loves you and I know you love him. You both need to be honest with each other and see where it leads. You guys have been apart for a little over five years. Don't let him walk away again and don't send him away again." Chase patted Ashley on the cheek.

"I know. Everything has just happened so

quickly. I will talk to him. Right now we all need to concentrate on the success of this operation." Ashley smiled tight lipped as they headed back inside for the continuation of the meeting.

"Chase go ahead, I'm stopping by the restroom."

"I'll save your seat." Chase saluted her as he walked down the corridor to the conference room.

Ashley stared at her reflection in the mirror, fully expecting an answer from herself to emerge. "Could she risk her heart once more on Anthony? Would he vanish again with no explanations? That simply would not be fair to A. J., and she had to put A. J. first. She decided to make a quick call to A. J. before going back to the meeting. It might be awhile before she could talk to him again. She dialed the number and waited and it rang and rang........

"Hey", A. J. answered on the fifth ring.

"Hello sweetie, I love you, and Hey is no way to answer the phone."

"I know momma. Aunt Lynn said I could answer cause it was you. How did she know that it was you?"

"Aunt Lynn has caller I.D. on their phone. It shows up the number and she knew the number was mine. What have you been doing?"

"Aunt Gina came by to see us and Uncle Morgan got mad cause I was hittin rocks with his goff clubs. He said I could have picked any of them except his big berfa or somethin like that........."

"Oh, no. Honey you need to use a stick or something, don't use Uncle Morgan golf clubs, it will break them, and they are very expensive." Ashley tried to cover her laughter.

"I miss you momma. When you comin home?" A. J. pouted.

"I will see you very soon, honey." Ashley promised. "I have to go now sweetie." Ashley headed out of the restroom toward the corridor.

"I love you momma."

"Honey, I love you too, I miss you and will see you soon." Ashley clicked the phone shut and walked straight into the hard chest of Anthony.

"Who do you love, Ashley?" Anthony's eyes

were hard as steel and piercingly angry as he glared down into her face.

"Please...." She raised anguished eyes. "I'd rather we discussed this later. You don't understand." Her tone was pained, carrying thousands of regrets.

"You want me to stand here and pretend I didn't hear you tell another man you loved him, missed him and that you would see him soon. The sound of your voice was like caramel and the glint in your eyes of sunshine. I remember last night and this morning you screamed my name over and over and you said you loved me. Was that an act? I thought it was good for you too," he murmured.

"I can't do this, right now," she cried, the calm composure she'd maintained so far with him this morning now in total tatters. "I'm sorry. Last night was beautiful but........." Her eyes pleaded. "I want to close the door on it for now, Tony. We have to concentrate on the operation."

"I guess you'd better spell that out for me. Ashley, do you only want the door closed on what we shared in the past? Or do you also want it closed on any future we might have together? Or are you just a two-timing slut and sleep around these days? Does closing the door for now mean........until you can see the lover boy you called again on your phone or what?"

She took a deep breath. Her eyes looked sick but she said the words. "There is no future for us, Tony."

It was a flat, unequivocal denial of the bond he'd felt with her – a bond that had spanned seven years for him and would probably haunt the rest of his life.

"You're damn right about that one sweetheart." Anthony snarled.

"Tony, you don't understand......" Ashley begged, wanting to explain everything but unable to do so right now.

Instead of being honest with his emotions, his gaze flicked to hers in savage derision. "There's nothing else left to be said..... I got what I wanted from you last night and it wasn't too bad. Now you can go back to your lover and compare notes."

Her cheeks were burning. Before she could stop

herself she reached up and slapped Anthony hard across the face. "You're an ass and you don't have a clue what you're talking about."

Anthony's smile was menacing as he glowered down at her. His hand automatically reaching up and touching his cheek, it still stung from the imprint of her hand.

"That is the last time you will ever raise your hand in anger to me, for the next time I shall strike you back. I should consider myself lucky to have maintained my freedom. And to think, I was going to ask a whore to be my wife." Anthony stared through her with pure hatred in his eyes.

"Enjoy your freedom and all that goes along with it….." Ashley said softly and simply turned and walked away.

CHAPTER THIRTEEN

Ashley didn't go back into the conference room. She was in no mood to face Anthony, Chase, Grayson, Roberto or any other man. Chase could give her the details of what she missed and what she needed to do before tonight. Having retrieved the jeep from the parking lot, she drove home to the cottage on the beach.

The heavy rain pelting the windshield was making it difficult to see and the wind had picked up causing the jeep to rock unsteadily. She turned on the radio to check the status of the hurricane. Projected landfall was still seven to nine hours away and would be at least a hundred and twenty five miles down the coast. They would experience some heavy rain and winds from the outer bands from now until midnight. An all craft advisory was in effect as well, she knew this would have a negative impact on the operation tonight.

Heart of Jaded Justice

The view of the gulf from the sliding glass doors of the cottage patio reminded her of the view from her and Anthony's home years ago. She wondered if Anthony had noticed the same. He'd barged into her life last night, uninvited; and demanded rekindling of a relationship between them. She had been a more than willing participant in their lovemaking over and over through the night and early morning hours. "How could he have called me a two-timing slut and a whore?" she asked herself aloud. If he had truly loved her, he would never have accused her of being a slut and he would have waited for the answers to his questions. His statements had hurt so badly that she had told him there would never be a future for them. The bond she felt for Tony had to be a fantasy. The only bond that truly existed was the fact that he was A. J.'s father. Never mind the fact that she still loved him. She would be damned if she would tell him that now.

And the final insult was his freedom. It was pointless to struggle for understanding when she clearly had no understanding of him. Tony valued his freedom so much that is was time to close the door forever. She would complete the operation tonight and leave for D.C. on the first plane out tomorrow, if she could get a flight to D.C. on Saturday. She had so wanted to bring A. J. down here for a vacation. Brenda and Chase would really enjoy spending time with them both. She had not been able to spend very much time with Brenda since she had arrived. Well, maybe Anthony would take his freedom to another part of the world and she could bring A. J. down for a vacation. After she returned Patrick to Aunt Lynn and Uncle Morgan as she promised.

Ashley walked upstairs to the bedroom, trying to still her racing heart. She rested both her hands on the dresser and took a deep, steadying breath. The sight of the rumpled bed made her weak at the knees. The scent of Tony's cologne still clung in the room like an intoxicating drug; it filled her senses and made her head spin out of control.

"Get a hold of yourself, Ashley Cameron," she whispered. "You're beyond this. Act like it." She threw back her head and looked into the mirror, only to turn away as a wave of pain crashed through her body with the force of a hurricane.

She could do this. And she had to remember that Tony's actions had spoken volumes about his feelings for her. He considered her a slut and he wanted his freedom. She would be happy to assure he had the latter.

You're lying, a voice inside her head whispered.

She might be, but it was the only way she was going to survive, and she had A. J. to think about. Ashley glanced at the clock on the night stand, it was four-thirty.

She could grab a quick shower, get dressed for tonight and drive back into town to visit with Brenda while she waited for Chase.

She dried off from the steaming shower, wrung the water from her hair, and then toweled the massive length partially dry. She decided to just let it dry naturally. Pulling on a black short sleeved V-neck pullover shirt with jeans and boots, she hurried downstairs. Ashley checked the clip and safety on her gun before clipping it and her phone on her belt. She snatched on a black sweatshirt hooded jacket before grabbing her purse and getting in the Jeep.

The surveillance guys probably thought she had lost her mind to run in and out so quickly. They simply smiled and waved at her comings and goings.

"You look like hell." Brenda's cheerful observation welcomed her as she opened the door.

"Thanks. I'm glad to know you don't hold back on the compliments."

"You don't want polite observations out of me. You want the truth."

Ashley snorted. "Both, Maybe? If that is possible?" She shrugged out of her sweatshirt and placed it on the counter.

"So your day went that well?" Brenda quietly asked. Seeing the warning in her eyes, she glanced around the room. "Come on in sweetie, and sit down before you fall down."

"Oh, Brenda. I have screwed everything up." Tears pricked at her eyelids as Ashley sobbed and relayed the whole night and day's events to her best friend.

"You slapped him again, today?" Brenda asked.

"Yes, I just got so angry when he called me a two-timing slut and a whore. I couldn't tell him that it was A. J. on the phone. And what right does he have to act this way after everything he did." Ashley swallowed back more tears.

"Oh, Ashley. You have to tell him the truth. Don't let him walk away again without knowing the full truth." Brenda smiled reassuringly.

"I do love him, he just makes me crazy and I have to think about A. J. What if I tell him everything and he walks out on A. J. That's not fair to him."

"Honey, not fair is hiding the truth from A. J. You said yourself he has been asking questions lately. Those questions will have to be answered. Let A. J. decide for himself if he wants to see Anthony or not. Better yet, if Anthony wants to meet his son, let them meet and get acquainted before you tell A. J. anything." Brenda advised.

"Brenda, I honestly don't know what I would do without you and Chase."

"Now, tell me how you feel. Do you want to

work things out with Anthony?"

"Yes, but I don't want to be hurt again. I don't think I could bear for him to just walk out again. I don't believe he wants me back."

"Did you ever find out why he walked out before?" Brenda asked.

"No, He asked me to let him explain and I refused to listen to him. I just assumed it was another woman."

"Well, don't you think he deserves for you to hear him out as well?"

The ringing of the telephone interrupted Ashley's reply. Brenda picked up the receiver.

"Yes, dear?"

"Yes, she's here."

"I don't know, I will tell her."

"Ashley, its Chase. He said to tell you to stay put until he gets here. He is on his way now."

"Okay, honey. I love you too. See you soon." Brenda hung up the phone.

Brenda glanced up at the grandfather clock. It

was six-ten.

"Let's go into the kitchen and make something quick for dinner. I am sure Chase will be hungry and you need to eat before going out to work tonight as well."

Ashley followed Brenda into the kitchen. "Did Chase sound angry on the phone?"

"He sounded more concerned than angry." Brenda busied herself unwrapping the chicken breasts she had grilled earlier for the garlic and butter linguini. She also made plates of sliced tomatoes, topped with red onion, thinly sliced mozzarella, and topped with fresh basil. She sprinkled a little olive oil and topped each with balsamic vinegar.

"My personal life really needs to stay on hold, until after the operation tonight. I don't want any of us to be distracted by what is going on between me and Anthony." Ashley broke apart the romaine lettuce and was rinsing it in the sink.

Brenda gave Ashley a sympathetic smile. The girls continued talking as they prepared the salads and placed a frozen loaf of garlic bread in the oven to bake.

"Did I tell you that A. J. used my uncle's golf clubs to hit rocks?"

Brenda laughed. "You're kidding?"

"No, I'm afraid not. Instead of "Big Bertha" A. J. called it big berfa or something. Leave it to my son to pick the most expensive club in the bag to hit rocks with. I will have to buy Uncle Morgan a new set when I get back home."

The bread was just coming out of the oven when Chase drove up.

Chase came in and kissed Brenda, while dropping his and Ashley's briefcases on the bar.

"You left in such a hurry, you forgot your briefcase."

"I'm so sorry, Chase. Anthony and I got in another argument when I came out of the restroom and I just couldn't stand to sit in the same room with him."

"He was like a bear with a sore head. He cornered me up after the meeting and wanted to know who you were screwing and how long it had been going on? Said you were on the phone and he heard you telling the guy how much you loved him, missed him and you would see him soon." Chase took a slice of the bread layered with five different cheeses and devoured it as they all sat down to eat.

"What did you tell him?" Ashley asked.

"I told him he would have to discuss that with you. I knew the minute he started barking about the man that you must have been on the phone with A. J. The green-eyed monster has devoured his soul whether you know it or not."

"He called me a two-timing slut and a whore!" Ashley screeched.

"Well, his left cheek had the distinct imprint of little fingers. I am guessing that you slapped him again?" Chase smirked.

"I couldn't help myself, he said he was glad to have his freedom and that he was glad he hadn't asked a whore to be his wife." Ashley retorted.

"Well, I hope you two don't start fighting tonight. We have enough bad guys to fight without enemies in the camp. We have to be at the Aztec Chemicals crossroads at seven thirty sharp. You got the gist of everything today; I will fill you in on a few more details on the way over there. Several of the units are already set up and pulling surveillance as we speak." Chase quickly finished off the last bite of his salad.

He slapped Brenda on the butt. "Thanks sweetheart, dinner was great. I'm heading upstairs to shower and change. Ashley, be ready to go when I get back down, we don't have long."

Brenda and Ashley cleaned up the kitchen. Ashley could tell that Brenda was worried.

"I'll make sure nothing happens to Chase."

"You know I always worry when he goes out on these details. I shudder every time the phone rings, so afraid of getting that phone call. You and Chase worked together for a long time. You know how each other thinks. I am really glad that you are back working with him on this one." Brenda hugged Ashley tight.

"I promise you, everything will be okay. The operation will go as planned and we will all return home safely." Ashley reassured her friend, hiding her own fears deep inside.

A short time later, Chase descended the stairs whistling the old *Casablanca* Tune, *As Time Goes By*.

"Where is Craig?"

"Are you kidding? It is Friday night; your son has a date tonight."

"The big boobed, blonde, bimbo that you don't like?" Chase laughed.

"You know I don't like her. She just isn't his type." Brenda pouted.

"Honey, he is almost seventeen years old. I think her type is just what he likes right now." Chase laughed.

"She is way too controlling, she burns his phone up constantly; if not calling then e-mailing, texting, all clingy, jealous and immature." Brenda stood arms crossed.

"And you were never that way with me, not even a little jealous?" Chase teased Brenda.

"No. Well, maybe a little. Anyway, I told him he had to be home by midnight."

"Does that go for me too?" Chase grinned at his wife.

"I wish I could make those demands of you, but I know you must work until you are finished. Just return home safely. And, please call me when it's over and let me know that all of you are okay and in one piece." Brenda kissed Chase full on the lips and hugged him tightly.

"Hey, you're not usually this mushy and weepy. What's wrong?" Chase asked, his smile quickly fading into a grimace.

"Nothing, honey." Just hurry home, I love you. I love you too, Ash. I fixed you guys several thermoses of hot coffee, and there are bags of snacks as well. Don't forget to grab them when you leave, I thought you might need them." Brenda waved them bye and headed upstairs.

"Bye, Brenda. She still doesn't like to watch you leave for work, does she?"

Chase replied. "No, she doesn't. It is harder for her since Craig has gotten older and he is gone too. She's here in this big house all alone, empty nest syndrome."

"A. J. is still so young, I'm not looking forward to his being a teenager and dating either. I can't image him all grown up. He is still my baby. Of course he would argue that point. He thinks he is all grown up. If he acts anything like his father, I will be in for years of pure hell."

"Mothers! You both worry too much. We need to get going. There were a few changes in plans. I'll brief you on the way. Grab our briefcases, would you?"

"Sure." Ashley grabbed their briefcases and the bags of snacks Brenda had made for them. She took the snacks because she loved her dearly, knowing full well they would be too stressed to eat anything.

"It is six-forty-five pm. We have just enough time to make it, if we hurry." Chase said as he pulled the door closed and locked it behind them, after setting the security alarm.

CHAPTER FOURTEEN

Lightning streaked the sky as the rain came down in torrential downpours. The wind had picked up significantly as they made their way to their assigned location. Roads were already beginning to wash out and some power outages were already being reported.

"Chase, do you really think Anthony is in as deep uncover as he thinks with Martinelli?"

"No, why do you ask that now?" Chase glanced over at Ashley.

"I don't know. Just this gut feeling I have that tonight may be a set-up. This is the line of work we have chosen. Our responsibilities supersede all bonds it seems it has always been that way." Ashley said quietly.

'Well, there is nothing we can do at this point, but keep our eyes open and alert. We are too close to really making a difference and stopping the Martinelli Drug Cartel forever."

"Or eliminating one of us forever. And did you notice the FBI Director left really early today? I still can't place where he knows me from." Ashley shook her head in puzzlement.

"Now, Ashley that is no way to be thinking. Don't you think everything that has happened with Anthony and seeing him again after all these years just has your nerves on edge? And maybe Mr. FBI had business to attend to… He is the director of the FBI you know. He may just remember some case you worked, you have worked everywhere in six states!"

"Oh, I am sure that is it…..Where are we stationed at?" Ashley asked as they pulled off the highway onto a small dirt lane across from the Chemical Plant.

"Just down the road a little way." Chase laughed. "Oh, I knew there was one little detail I forgot to relay to you. There is a power company bucket truck and clothes for us to change into. Hard hats and all the fancy gear; we did make a few adaptations to the tool belts, they still have the wire cutters, and knife but we added a couple of IEDs - low impact ones just to blow doors and a couple of hand grenades. If things go haywire, the Power Company will shut the power off and we will be ready to enter under the pretense of fixing the lines. With the current weather conditions that will cause no alarms as there are already outages occurring."

"Okay, that is one profession I haven't tried to emulate lately." Ashley laughed. "Will I get to strap on a tool belt and climb the power poles?"

"Let's hope not, you would fall and knock yourself out, as well as taking out the power in a whole city block, you just get to wear the tool belt." Chase jokingly replied.

They got out of the Jaguar and changed into the power company cover-all type suits. Ashley bound her hair on top of her head and pulled on a cap backwards. Luckily the gash to her forehead was low enough that the hat didn't touch. A black van approached with headlights out, just as they climbed up inside the bucket truck.

"That will be Roberto, Greg and Grayson." Chase said at Ashley's apprehensive look.

"What's cooking?" asked Roberto in his usual

upbeat manner. Grayson and Greg simply waved and shook their heads.

Roberto and Grayson got out of the van and slid the panel doors open, revealing the surveillance monitoring system. There was so much electronic equipment flashing and beeping that it looked like a NASA launch control room as Ashley exited the Bucket Truck and peered inside. There were audio and visual monitors displaying the events as they occurred inside the plant.

She immediately spotted Anthony on the first monitor, standing in an office in front of a massive sized desk. She couldn't see the man behind the desk as Anthony obscured the vision.

Monitor Two was displaying shrimp boats bobbing up and down in the bay with much velocity due to the high waves.

Monitor Three showed the two entrance gates with their security guards on duty. Both were CIA operatives that had overtaken the actual guards after shift change, taking their clothes, I.D. badges and weapons.

The actual guards were in the back of another panel van headed to the old airport for interrogation.

Monitor Four displayed the inside of the warehouse. A lot of movement from forklifts placing pallets of containers in rows just inside the roll down gates, to what appeared to be a full lab enclosed in a glass cubicle.

The last monitor showed the whole warehouse front facing the bay water. She counted eight men with what appeared to be automatic weapons strapped across their chests, canvassing this stretch of water front. The monitors were displaying blurred views due to the heavy rains.

Roberto pointed to the last monitor and indicated that these eight men had just arrived in that area, so the shipment must be on its way soon.

Grayson jumped as the printer started spitting out its newest information. Greg peeled the newest sheet off and handed it to Grayson as he turned to type a reply.

Grayson read aloud........"Florida Marine Patrol has just identified twenty ships of unknown origin about six miles out from St. Andrews Bay. The ships are staggered in patterns of five each approximately one half mile behind each other. Projected knots, factored with the high waves and wind will have the first five arriving in the Bay at approximately twenty-one hundred hours, with the others arriving at thirty minute intervals."

Ashley looked down at her watch. "Eight-forty five pm. That means the ships we be entering the port at nine, only fifteen minutes."

She glanced back up at the first monitor and saw Anthony exiting the office following closely behind Martinelli. They were heading down the long corridor to the warehouse area.

"Damn, they are staggered too far apart and their not all coming in together in groups due to the rough seas. There is barely enough time in between." Chase muttered. "Greg get that information out now to every operative we have in the field working this operation, make sure the seal team copies the transmission, it will be essential that they know when to detonate the explosives."

"Yes, sir. I am working on it right now." Greg continued typing and talking on the walkie at the same time.

"Ashley get in the bucket truck, I am sure we will have to take the power out and go in........" Chase grabbed a couple of the radios and one of the laptops and battery-packed monitors and tossed them up into the Bucket Truck.

Swallowing back the hurt and bitterness clinging to her throat, she began to study the diagrams. Breathe, she ordered herself. Concentrate on the task at hand. Forget the past.

She was repeating this mantra in her head when she realized they had approached their designated location.

Chase steered the truck down a dirt path adjacent to the power lines which was barely wide enough to maneuver to a good surveillance location high on top of the coconut grove covered ledge. A service road that led straight down to the east gate entrance of the Chemical Plant was directly in front of them. They were in a perfect position looking down on the bay front yet camouflaged and unseen.

Ashley's fingers stiffened slightly on the service weapon at her side then relaxed. She checked her AK-47 assault rifle; peering through the low light, variable intensity illuminated sight. If she had to use it from here, it would be like sending up a flare confirming their location. She stared out the windows of the truck watching the rain pelting down and the wind wildly whipping the palm trees from side to side.

Chase swiveled around in the driver seat, reaching behind him and tossing the laptop and binoculars to Ashley.

"Get it up and running as quickly as you can." Chase barked as he glanced down at his Rolex, reading eight-fifty five pm. I knew you would not stay with Greg and work the communication center, so I didn't even go there. But, keep Greg informed."

"Sorry." She shot him a sheepish smile. "Anyway, look at these surveillance shots. The CIA sharp shooters are already in position on the roof and eight already on the inside. The DEA and FBI boys are on the west corridor with the ATF and SWAT guys in place on the east. The seal team radar is flashing green so they are ready to go from the shrimp boats. The Customs group has the North corridor blocked and secured.

"Ships are two miles out now, repeating; ships are two miles from shore." Greg's voice was clear and level over the police radio.

"All right let's get, "Operation Sundown" up and running, just waiting on Anthony. Chase picked up his walkie and called Grayson and Roberto with the same information.

Everyone was in their assigned locations and "on ready" waiting to hear the code phrase from Anthony.

Ashley sat next to Chase wearing night-vision goggles, silently scanning the whole terrain below them. She slid the goggles down to her neck and started looking at the portable monitor, which scanned each of the five locations intermittently. Martinelli and Anthony were stopped near the end of the corridor. The software had finally loaded for the wire Anthony was wearing; the weather was delaying all of the computerized equipment by minutes. All observed movements and sounds were running almost a minute and four seconds behind real life. That didn't seem like a lot but in a real life or death situation; it was an eternity. Ashley slowly turned up the sound to hear the transmissions from his body microphone.

Martinelli strode easily down the last section of the corridor, looking sleek as a panther. Anthony was motioning toward the door to the warehouse. Six of the Martinelli men followed closely, all strapped with assault rifles across their chest.

At the end of the foyer, just as they were about to open the double steel doors that led into the warehouse; Martinelli stopped pushed a button on a small remote attached to his key ring and a panel slid back revealing a large door immediately to their right.

"Victor, would you like to see what is behind door number one?" Adrianno Martinelli unlocked the door and gestured for Victor to enter ahead of him.

Heart of Jaded Justice

Ashley adjusted the monitor trying to display a different angle of the room as it was dimly lit and casting shadows. She could barely make out a silver haired man in a business suit sitting in semidarkness. His face illuminated only by the lighthouse in the bay flickering through the window behind him. Ashley did not recognize his face; he was a totally unknown quantity.

Miniature cameras had been installed in the walls, fixtures and fittings in the office suites and other parts of the warehouse by the CIA. This particular room was nowhere in any of the blueprints they had utilized for the operation so they were relying solely on the audio and video wire Anthony was wearing. The audio was receiving strongly but satellite feed for the video was being delayed due to the storm. Ashley wondered why this room was not depicted in any of the blueprints.

Only Anthony and Adrianno had entered the room accompanied by two of the guards; the other four guards remained vigil outside the closed door.

CHAPTER FIFTEEN

Anthony entered the room warily looking from side to side, his weapon down at his side, just underneath the cover of his jacket. Using all of his training, Anthony, quickly assessed the situation while keeping his distance from Adrianno, his two guards, and the unknown subject. He knew instinctively this was a set up.

"It is a nice night and *Way, Way Past Sundown on the Horizon*"

"Good evening, Mr. Victor Shayne, or should I say AGENT?" the silver haired man asked in almost a raspy whisper.

Adrianno immediately ordered the two guards to secure Victor.

Anthony sprung forward, slamming into both guards with the full force of his body. His left hand was like rigid steel, smashing against the cartilage of one of the guards throat, twisting the larynx enough to disable, not to kill. The guard let out a loud scream of pain and surprise before landing unconscious on the floor. Simultaneously, with his right hand, Anthony cracked the Beretta against the back of the other guards head, aiming with precision. The guard slumped to the floor, still and lifeless but Anthony had lost his gun in the struggle. He quickly made a run for the door, but it would not open; as he turned Adrianno drug a jagged knife across the base of his throat, blood started trickling down his neck and across his chest. The silver haired fox aimed a .45 directly at his forehead then with one swift movement silver fox cracked him across the skull and in the mouth with the piece, blood spewed everywhere. Adrianno ordered him to kick his gun across the floor.

    Silver Fox threw Adrianno a large role of insulated electrical wire, as he picked up Anthony's Beretta. Working quickly, Silver Fox held the gun on Anthony as Adrianno bound Anthony's hands and feet so that the more he moved the tighter the knots would become. They drug the semi-conscious Anthony to a chair in front of the huge window overlooking the warehouse.

"He is an impressive specimen", Silver Fox said dispassionately. "Powerful -- almost like a coiled spring."

Adrianno spun to one side, chuckling. "He is ruthless, isn't he?"

"How long has he worked for you?"

"Four years now, four years of promoting him to run my overseas operations, only to discover from you tonight that he is a damn fed."

Anthony lifted his head, eyes squinted. "Adrianno, you bastard!" He tried to pull his hands up, grimaced as the thin wires cut into his wrists.

Silver Fox turned back to Adrianno, before speaking to Anthony. "We're going to play a little game here called Truth or Consequences. You see this room is like a sanctuary; it is completely soundproof and bulletproof, so your Calvary will not be rushing in to your rescue. You tell me the truth, or you face the consequences. Let's start with a simple question: Who are you, and what do you know?"

"Who the fuck are you, you old bastard?"

Anthony snarled through bloody teeth.

"I am your worst nightmare, Mr. Agent. Now once again who are you and what do you know?"

"Fuck you!" Anthony yelled. "I'm not done yet? He struggled against the restraints wincing.

"No," Silver Fox said with a smile. "Neither am I, leaning down to breathe right in Anthony's face."

Anthony spit; saliva hit Silver Fox in the face. "Fuck you!" He shouted.

Silver Fox wiped at the spit with the sleeve of his expensive suit. "I'll ask you one more time, and if I don't get a truthful answer -- operative word being truthful-- I'll be forced to use this." He walked over to the desk, placed the .45 on the desk, opened the top drawer, pulled out a .357 and held it up for display.

Fox could see him shifting his ankles, his wrists, testing the restraints for weaknesses, but there were none. "You see, Mr. Agent, I want to give you something that will really mean something to you. I am Lewis S. Fox and I am the one you have wanted to meet for many, many years. You see, I AM the Godfather of the Dixie Mafia".

Anthony's head was buzzing, blood was oozing from his face, everything was fuzzy, and he struggled to maintain consciousness." He attempted to puzzle out what Fox was saying.

"Oh, I have no intention of killing you, not quickly anyway." said Fox coolly. "You're a brave fellow; I've seen you face down death fearlessly. Death doesn't frighten you, which is one of the things that makes you so good at what you do. You are very good at fucking up my business! Do you have any idea how much you have cost me in the past fifteen years? How many shipments of drugs and guns you have commandeered?"

"I don't know you." Anthony stated defiantly.

"You see this pretty little piece here? Real nice, .357 Smith and Wesson. Well, let me tell you what is so special about her. The medical examiner down here has been on my payroll for twenty years, we actually took care of a little personal matter for him years ago. Once the deed was done, his soul belonged to me. You would really be surprised how many law enforcement officials I own." he gave a derisive laugh.

Anthony's face went pale; he knew who this man was now.

Fox waved the .357 in the air, opening the chamber and giving her a spin. "As I was saying, these are very special bullets; you see I collected them from Medical Examiner Sloan after he dug them out of your fellow officer's dead carcasses; you know the ones who would not sell out! M.E. Sloan didn't mind tampering with evidence and substituting bullets, always providing me with the real thing. I had them reloaded with a little scrap as hollow points. Yes, I can see by the look on your face, Copper; you know what a hollow point does. On impact it explodes and sends shards of metal racing all through your body; ripping through muscle, organs and bones." Fox gave a derisive laugh.

"So I ask you one more time, and consider very carefully before you either refuse to answer or lie to me: Who are you?"

"Fuck you!"

Fox fired the .357, Anthony groaned in anguish; blood started to drench his left side.

Fox approached, leaned over Anthony and spoke slowly in a raspy low voice. "How does it feel to have the same bullet in you that came out of your copper friends head; you know the one in the apartment complex parking lot? In the mid to late 1990s, he found out too much and just would not take my money and shut his fool damn mouth."

"Why?" mumbled Anthony glaring at Adrianno, in excruciating pain. "Why do it?"

"I need to know if this is a set-up. It is too late for me to turn all this cargo around, Victor or whoever the hell you are. I promised you if you ever fucked me that there would not be enough body bags for all the damn pieces you would be in." Adrianno demanded an answer, while grabbing Anthony's torn bloody shirt and twisting the wound site.

Anthony tried to focus, blood was still trickling down his neck; he tried to ignore the stabbing pain and stay conscious. If he gave in, it would all be over. Maybe, just maybe, Adrianno still had some doubts as to his identity. It could buy some time. "Adrianno, I don't know what Fox is talking about, I have been loyal to you, and I'm no traitor." His side wound was oozing thick and hot as Adrianno disgustedly released his hold.

Fox fired the .357 again this time striking Anthony in the right shoulder.

"You fucking bastard." Anthony was so weak it came out as a agonizing whisper.

Fox was standing over him smiling. "I ask you again, how does it feel to have the same bullet in you that came out of your cop friend's head, you know the officer that stopped the liquor store robbers? In the 90s, he found out too much and just would not take my money and shut his fool damn mouth either. It was real easy for me to have them both taken out!"

"Don't you think that is enough? He doesn't know shit or he would have given it up by now. I have more profitable business that needs my immediate attention." Adrianno said disgustedly.

"Oh, but I have a few more weapons with special ammo like these reserved only for cops." Fox nodded back toward the gun safe in the corner.

All of a sudden, everything around them went black. A small humming sound indicated a power generator was kicking on.

"The storm must have taken the power out." Adrianno said.

Anthony's breathing was getting shallower and he felt himself fading away. He wanted to close his eyes just for a few seconds, he felt really cold......

In the distance, far, far away he heard Adrianno asking....

"Why do you think he is a fed anyway, Lewis? He has been with me for four years now and I made him prove himself. Federal Agents don't perform murder for hire, now do they? I saw the bodies….." Adrianno shook his head in disbelief.

Fox chuckled. "There is a reason, you work for me. I am the only one with the brains to handle the big five for drugs, guns, prostitution, murder……you name it, it is mine. I am Lewis S. Fox, the GODFATHER of the Dixie Mafia, don't forget it……. Organized Business not Organized Crime is what I call it, for all of the great states of Alabama, Georgia, Florida, Mississippi and Louisiana!"

Fox smiled again, looking like the cat that swallowed the canary. "I own the Director of the FBI. Lawrence southern belle of a daughter has been my wife for almost twenty years. Now, open that door and bring your guards in immediately. Let the bastard bleed out, dispose of his body, and clean up this shit in here. We have twenty million dollars' worth of drugs and guns sitting right outside that window, just floating in the bay. You will deliver what you promised. I will take care of my friend Lawrence later for waiting until the last minute to share this bastard's true identity!" Fox calm threat left no room for argument.

With that Fox walked to the back of the room and pulled a book out of the bookcase, the wall to the side opened up revealing a tiny hallway. He slithered inside, and was gone as the wall closed shut with a thud.

CHAPTER SIXTEEN

11 Minutes Earlier

"Chase, Tony is burnt. We have to move in immediately." Ashley's voice was surprisingly, steady and controlled, even though she was dying a thousand deaths inside. Anthony had been cut, she continued monitoring.

"Chase, hurry! That bastard has shot Anthony." Ashley let out a bloodcurdling scream, "Fuck it; Chase, he just shot him again!"

"All units move in immediately.... Operation is at CODE RED" Greg was transmitting rapidly and repeatedly over all scanners and radios.

Chase drove the power company truck at lightning speed down the trail almost toppling it over twice. The dirt rutted trail was not meant for a truck of this size. He rammed it straight through the exterior fencing. "Where is the room Tony is in Ash? I know it is not on any of the blueprints, but I need your best guess to get us as close as possible."

"I don't know!" Ashley snapped, shaking her head back and forth violently.

"Think Ashley, think! Chase stated firmly.

"It has to be in the back facing the bay, the window behind the silver haired man had the Lighthouse beam flashing on and off through it, that would be the south east corner by the bay!" Ashley pulled on the bullet proof vest and strapped her AK and tightened her tool belt, clipping her .45 on the side of it.

Within moments, there was an immense explosion; the front part of the warehouse had turned into a fireball, as well as the back left side facing the bay. With steely concentration Chase drove the truck straight through the fire which had taken out the exterior wall. The truck came to a rest midway in the lobby, adjacent to the corridor leading to the back warehouse.

Ashley's thoughts were frantic. She jumped out of the truck running down the corridor straight toward the warehouse area with Chase on her heals.

Jesus Christ! Bullets were streaking by so closely they were whistling in her ears.

Chase caught a glimpse of the array of large weapons that lay abandoned at the end of the last corridor. That told him his enemies had pinpointed their location. When you are outnumbered, go on the offensive. His instincts told him to fire first and take out as many as he could. Roberto and Grayson took the right corridor and he and Ashley went straight. Both teams left a path of bloody moaning and dead bodies in their wake. Suddenly there was an enormous crash from directly overhead, then another. Minutes later, near the end of the corridor; the screech of metal scraping against metal was heard. A trapdoor was visible as the ceiling appeared to open. A rope ladder fell downward and Chase and Ashley put their backs to the wall using hand motions for communication.

Four Cartel men scampered down the ladder.

Just as the last one's feet hit the floor; Chase and Ashley cut them all in half with a rush of gunfire from their AK-47 assault rifles.

There was a shout from above, it was Roberto and Grayson. "Come on, let's go! We got you clear up here."

Ashley swung the weapon over her shoulder, holding the canvas strap to her chest as she climbed the ladder to the second floor, Grayson grabbing her and pulling her upward and behind some containers. The night vision goggles were clouding up from perspiration and she couldn't see well.

Just as Chase was being pulled upward by Roberto, she heard an agonizing scream. Chase had been hit. She tried to go to him but Grayson would not release his hold on her arm.

"I got you, my man." Roberto told Chase while dragging him to safety; then reaching into his tool belt, pulling a pin with his teeth before throwing the grenade down to the second floor.

"I'm okay; it's just a leg wound. Go, Go, and get

those bastards!" he ordered them. Chase leaned back with his weapon aimed ahead, concealed behind rows of containers.

"Come on, let's go! That grenade will only slow them down." Roberto ordered.

"Chase, will you be okay here?" Ashley was torn, not wanting to leave Chase but needing to help Tony.

"Get the hell out of here and get them, Ash." Chase leaned forward and aimed his gun directly behind her, taking out two more of the cartel men. One of them got off a shot and it pierced Ashley in the upper thigh.

The three of them ran down the corridor until they saw the four gunmen standing at the end. Roberto, Grayson and Ash immediately hit the wall for cover. The four guards had not seen them.

"They may be guarding the room Tony is in" Ashley whispered, gritting her teeth and tying the strap from her shoulder holster around the wound on her thigh. She peered around Roberto and saw a man fully armed, approaching through the warehouse doors on the other side of the guards. She could hear a chopper taking off from the roof overhead.

"On the count of three, Roberto take out the two guards on the right, I will get the two on the left and Ashley nail that bastard walking toward them." Grayson commanded.

"One, two, three."

The explosion of gunshots was followed immediately by the sound of steel hitting steel as the rounds went through the guards and hit the steel wall behind them. The four guards collapsed lifeless to the floor, the last man that approached them was writhing on the floor, a .45 in his hand, as Ashley had zeroed in on him with gunfire.

"Throw your weapon and identify yourself?" Ashley demanded, approaching the subject. Her .45 aimed at his head.

"Hey, bitch! Long time, no see. I know you missed me!" mocked Ricky Martinelli, leveling a .45 straight at her chest. "You pussy ass bitch don't have what it takes to pull that trigger, you would miss me too much, I on the other hand can…." Ricky snarled pulling his gun up level with her head.

"Yeah, I missed doing this; you fucking asshole!" Heart pounding, she fired, sending a bullet straight through his skull.

The panel door just behind Ashley opened as she fired her weapon. "Ricky, my sweet child, You have killed my Ricky." Adrianno let out a tortured scream. His aim was too good, too close, another explosion filled the air.

The bullet tore into the Kevlar vest with the impact of a hundred powerful fists slamming her in the chest. Ashley slowly went down, winded and unable to move.

More explosions. Bullets flying. Adrianno fell inside the open doorway, and crumpled to the floor; the lighthouse beam passing over his dead body. Roberto kicked the dead body of Adrianno out of the way. Grayson helped Ashley up and got her inside the darkened room. She saw the chair where Tony sat slumped over in a pool of blood. "Oh, my God!" she whispered, her breathing coming out in sharp bursts.

"Oh, my God, Tony." Ashley ignored her pain and immediately went to Tony's side. She could smell the coppery scent of Tony's blood as she removed the wire cutters from her tool belt and gently cut the restraints around Anthony's feet and hands. Roberto eased him out of the chair and onto the floor. Tears filled her eyes as she placed her hand over Tony's wound to stop the bleeding. Immediately, Roberto added his own hands to Tony's chest, pressing his jacket into the wounds to stanch the flow of blood. "Tony, can you hear me?"

They could hear footsteps coming closer and closer.

"Greg, get us a medic up here ASAP, life flight will be needed." Roberto barked the order into the radio.

"Copy, they are already here and headed down to you now." "We got them all, DEA, Seal Team and ATF have control of all the ships and merchandise and are loading up to carry out the sting. CIA, DEA and FBI Agents have the entire Cartel in custody." Repeat, Operation Sundown on the Horizon is a success."

"I am going to check on Chase." Grayson quickly

exited out the doorway and down the corridor.

"Anthony, please talk to me, please." Ashley begged.

Anthony barely lifted his head, looked up at her and gave a very slight smile. "No, FBI." "No, FBI."

"What do you mean, No, FBI." Ashley asked getting weaker but holding on with everything she had. She could feel the blood oozing underneath her own vest.

"I love you." Anthony said, weakly.

"I have always loved you." Ashley said, weeping. "Please don't leave me again!"

"We got those bastards, this time; justice. I am so cold." Anthony said barely audible.

His chest was barely rising and falling as the medics arrived pulling Ashley away to stabilize Anthony before placing him on the stretcher and rushing him down the corridor to the awaiting life flight helicopter.

"I need to go with him…." Ashley let out an anguished sob, tears streaming down her blood smeared face. Then she drifted off, sliding pale and unconscious into a heap on the floor; as Roberto caught, and cradled her on his lap.

Grayson walked in bearing most of Chase weight. Chase had his arm draped around Grayson shoulder and neck as he couldn't walk without help, his whole right leg covered in blood. Two medics rushed over and took Chase from Grayson and began treating him.

"Oh, my God!" Chase looked over and saw Ashley lying still and unmoving in Roberto's lap.

A medic was lifting her limber arm, checking her wrist for a pulse. "We are going to need another stretcher, he called over the radio."

"Grayson, what the hell happened here?" Chase demanded.

"It was total chaos and confusion. When we got up here, we took the guards out in the hallway just as another man came bursting through the double steel doors from the warehouse. He had a .45 and Ashley used department protocol, demanding he identify himself. It was Ricky Martinelli! Ashley shot him in the head, just as the panel door was opening. Adrianno was exiting and saw her shoot Ricky; he shot Ashley at close range just as we opened up fire on him. Adrianno was too close and got her, through the vest. It all happened so quickly."

"Eleven minutes and forty-five seconds of pure bloody Hell. Ashley is right Justice is Jaded!" Chase said solemnly, watching the medic pushing the stretcher with Ashley's lifeless body down the corridor and out the doors to the waiting chopper.

"Roberto, go with her on the chopper." Chase murmured, flinching as the medic cut his pants to examine his bleeding leg.

"We are going to need another stretcher; this one has lost a lot of blood. Also, go ahead and notify Bay City Medical Center that they need to have the trauma unit ready, three officers incoming! It is a little farther away but has the closest and best trauma unit." The medic treating Chase called over his radio. Another medic arrived to assist with Chase.

Grief or relief, Chase had no idea what to feel. Relieved it was all over, and grief over the brutal assaults on his friends. "How bad are Ash and Tony?" He questioned Grayson.

"Tony is in really bad shape." Grayson shook his head. "I'm not sure about Ash."

"You ready to go?" the medic asked. "It is going to hurt when we lift you up on the stretcher."

"Grayson, go by my house and tell Brenda what is going on…. Tell her we are okay; before she hears or sees it on the news." Chase squeezed his eyes shut, grimacing in pain and they lifted him up on the stretcher.

Sirens shrieked from a distance, getting closer, as the helicopters carrying the last of the three officers lifted off from the roof of Aztec Chemicals. Blue lights, red lights, squad cars, and fire trucks looked tiny as Chase looked downward out the window of the chopper as it ascended. The swishing sounds of the blades overhead, being the last thing he remembered. The helicopter carrying Anthony landed on the pad atop Bay City Medical Center.

CHAPTER SEVENTEEN

It was a quarter after four in the morning, and Brenda was still pacing the pristine white floors of the waiting room outside of ICU. She closed her eyes tightly, and then slowly forced her eyes open. Lord, it hadn't all been a bad dream. She really was at St. Andrews Medical Center waiting for news on her husband, Ashley and Tony. All three had undergone surgery and were now in the unit. The doctor had come out to let her know that Chase had made it through surgery and was going to be fine. She had asked if he could provide her with updates on Ashley and Tony as they had no family there for them. The doctor said that Ashley came out of surgery fine but that Tony was still in the operating room. Oh, dear God, please let them all be okay.

When Grayson came and picked her up shortly after midnight, she was frantic. Craig came downstairs as

Grayson was telling her that Chase had been shot; along with Ashley and Anthony. He insisted he was coming with her, tears brimming in his eyes.

Brenda glanced at her son; sitting hunched over starring down at the floor tiles.

"Craig, we can go in and see your dad in about five minutes." Brenda said. She hoped that Chase was alert this time when they went in to see him. An hour earlier, he was still very groggy.

Craig stood up and walked out of the waiting room to the double doors of the ICU to wait beside his mom, never saying a word.

Brenda shook her head, studying her fingernails, which she'd been chewing mercilessly. She looked up to see two uniformed guards standing on either side of the Unit doors. There were also officers stationed down the corridor and one inside the waiting room. Grayson was like a shadow, quietly following them wherever they went.

Chase smiled weakly as Brenda and Craig walked up to his bed. "You guys don't have to look so happy to see me."

"Oh, Chase! We have been so worried." Brenda brushed the tears away as she bent over and kissed her husband on the cheek.

He reached up and brushed her springy red hair back from her ear and whispered, "I love you, sugar. It's all okay, now."

"Is it really okay, dad? Did you get all of them or will they come back after you again? There are cops everywhere in this hospital." Craig said almost in a whisper as he walked a little closer to the foot of his dad's bed.

"There is always a chance, son….. Just not much of one. We got the heavy hitters tonight, the ones that make a difference. We didn't leave anyone to come after us." Chase took a deep breath.

"Dad, hate to tell you this; but it's not night anymore. It is now five a.m. Saturday morning."

Chase attempted to whistle a little bit of *As Time Goes By*, and winced slightly.

Brenda and Craig both shook their heads and laughed.

"Dad, can I go across the hall and check on Aunt Ash?"

Chase nodded for his son to go and looked up at his wife. "How are Ashley and Tony?" Chase closed his eyes, swallowed hard. He remembered them taking Tony out and he was in really bad shape. He knew Ashley had been hit but she had her bullet proof vest on, so she should be okay.

"Ashley is out of surgery and is going to be okay. Tony has been in surgery for over four hours now, he is pretty messed up, doc says it is touch and go." Brenda whispered.

Chase swore long and low, and then took a deep breath. "Does Ashley know? Have you seen her?"

"She was still out of it at last visitation." "I asked the doctors to give me updates on all of you as I knew Ashley and Tony had no family here. Grayson has been our shadow, and Roberto hasn't left Ashley's side. The CIA has a man posted up at surgery with Tony as well." Brenda smiled thinly.

Chase's grip tightened on her hand as he

continued starring at her face. "Oh, angel, I love you and everything is going to be fine."

"Your Boss, Director Madison was here until about an hour ago. He asked me to let him know when you were awake. Said he had some things to take care of and would be back."

"I am sure he is still monitoring the remainder of the operation." Chase said quietly.

"Man, she is pissed!" Craig came rushing into the room. "Aunt Ash just cussed the doctor out and said she was fine and wanted out of the damn bed; demanding to know where you and Tony were…." "I told her you were across the hall with mom and that you were okay. She wasn't hearing any of it… kept yelling at the nurse to get that shit out of her arm, and pulling at her IV. Mr. Roberto told her to calm down."

"Craig, stay here with your dad. I will go see about Ashley, she can be a real handful at the best of times!" Brenda quietly exited the room and walked across the hall.

ICU - Room 4

"Ashley, how are you?" Brenda asked quietly as she walked up to Ashley's bed as Roberto gave her a grateful look and stepped just outside the door.

"Oh, Brenda. I have to check on Tony, tell them to let me go." Ashley murmured. She was so pale with dark circles under her eyes. Her breathing was heavy and agitated. "I am fine, I had my vest on, the bullet barely entered my body, it just hit an artery; I lost a lot of blood. They removed the slug that just grazed my thigh. I am okay, now." She pleaded with Brenda to get her out of the bed.

Brenda sat down gently at the foot of Ashley's bed and stroked her leg. "Sweetie, Tony is still in surgery. I have been keeping a check on all of you all night and this morning. The doctor has promised to let me know the minute the surgery is complete."

"Morning?" Ashley questioned in puzzlement.

"Yes, it is almost six a.m. on Saturday morning. You were in recovery a couple hours before they brought you to the unit."

Ashley leaned back against the pillows with her right arm across her forehead and her left one lying at her side with IV's attached. She shook her head, still trying to take it all in......... Saturday morning, the last she remembered it was late Friday night; they were in the warehouse corridor and she had shot Ricky Martinelli then his father Adrianno had shot her at close range penetrating her vest. It was all coming back.... They were in the office area at the warehouse where she found Tony, shot and bleeding, dying.. He didn't know he had a son. She closed her eyes to such thoughts.

"Do you feel like a visitor?" A short gray haired man with glasses quietly asked from just inside the doorway.

"Director Jones, please come in.... maybe you can tell all of them I am okay and get me out of here so I can check on Tony. I need to check on Tony...." Ashley solemnly stated.

"I have men posted upstairs with him, he is just coming out of surgery, he is however; in very critical condition. I will be honest with you Ms. Cameron; he suffered a knife and two gunshot wounds. He has a lot of internal injuries and lost a lot of blood. The next forty-eight hours will be touch and go; but Anthony is a fighter, I know he will pull through." Director Jones spoke softly from the side of Ashley's bed.

"I have to see him, I have to see him." Tears streamed down Ashley's face. Brenda gently squeezed her hand reassuringly.

"And you will see him soon, Ms. Cameron. I am here at Anthony's request. He explained to me your connection to Patrick and asked that I bring him to you after the operation was over if anything happened to him. He said you were related and would contact his family. Patrick is your cousin, correct?" Director Jones asked.

"Yes." Ashley stated barely above a whisper.

Director Jones stepped to the doorway and motioned with his hand. Two officers appeared, one on either side of Patrick.

"Patrick!" Ashley cried.

"Oh, Ashley. I am so sorry." Patrick rushed to

her bedside, face down on the bed, sobbing. "I know mom and dad have been so worried. I have been under protection, some guy told me you were here working the case. I knew you would get to the bottom of everything." He continued shaking as his body convulsed with a flood of tears.

She brushed her hand across the top of his spiked hair. "It's all okay now, baby." Ashley looked at Patrick's thin, drawn and faintly bruised face. He had lost weight and looked so pale. She noticed the wound almost healed under his eye.

"Director Jones, May I call his parents?" Ashley asked.

"Yes, but we have to discuss a few things first. He has to remain in protective custody, as well as you, Chase and his family and several other agents. His parents may come here; but you all have to stay in a safe house until all debriefings are finalized and Operation Sundown is officially complete. This entails the culmination of the sting operation which is still on-going. That aspect should be completed by midnight tonight and all those arrests made as well. You realize we still have many agents in the field working this operation." Director Jones was sitting in the chair next to Ashley's bed, staring intently at her; to assure her complete comprehension.

"What about Tony? And, my four and a half year old son is with Patrick's parents. Aunt Lynn and Uncle Morgan have been watching him for me to come here and work." Ashley was fidgeting with the sheet on the bed as she spoke.

"I didn't realize you had a son, Ms. Cameron. Let me know when you have contacted your aunt and uncle and I will have the CIA escort them to the safe house."

Ashley looked at Brenda with tears in her eyes and simply nodded to Director Jones.

"I have a suggestion to make." Brenda firmly spoke up.

"You are Mrs. Brady. Chase's wife, correct?" Director Jones inquired.

"Yes, sir. We have an extremely large two story home. There are four bedrooms upstairs and two downstairs. She explained exactly where the home was located. Can you utilize our home as the safe house?"

"Well, that is a little out of the ordinary; but it just might work. I will assign some agents to go by there and secure the place and get it ready. You will also have Grayson and Roberto attached to you twenty four seven. I have been advised that both Ashley and Chase will be released late this evening. I will instruct the agents to take you up to see Tony as soon as he is out of recovery." Director Jones thanked Brenda and advised Ashley to go ahead and make the call to her aunt and uncle.

Brenda smiled at Roberto as he entered the room when she was leaving to go across the hall and let Chase know their home had now become the Safe House for Operation Sundown.

ICU - Room 1

Brenda entered Chase's room and informed her husband of the news.

"Well, you have been complaining about how

empty the house felt. I guess you will not be able to say that by tonight, now will you?" Chase teased his wife.

"Cool." Craig piped in, thinking all of this was some form of entertainment now that he knew his dad was going to be okay.

Brenda just smiled as she snuggled up next to her husband on the hospital bed, taking his hand in hers and gently kissing his palm.

"Yuck, you guys are getting all mushy, get a room." Craig snorted.

"We are in a room of sorts!" Chase and Brenda Chuckled.

"I can't wait to see, A.J., can he stay in the room with me, since there are going to be so many people at our house, dad?"

Chase looked down at Brenda. "I don't see why not, if Ashley doesn't mind."

Chase and Brenda both continued looking at each other.....

All the secrets from the past would not be secret much past sundown on the horizon tonight!

CHAPTER EIGHTEEN

They didn't have any real close neighbors but, Brenda felt sure the nearest ones thought they were terrorists and that National Guard had landed at their home. Officers were stationed inside and out as she, Chase, Craig, Ashley and Patrick arrived in the black Cadillac shuttle bus just before sundown.

Roberto led the way with Grayson following behind.

The stars winked brightly in the evening sky just as the sun set on the horizon. All remnants of the storm having passed, leaving behind wet pavement littered with limbs and palm branches and a few loose garbage cans. Ashley stared into the evening sky in total silence. She was able to visit Tony only for a few minutes before being discharged from the hospital. Agents had taken her upstairs to his private room just as Director Jones had promised. He was hooked up to so many machines, looked ghostly pale and lifeless. The pain from her ribs cracked by Martinelli's bullet was nothing compared to the ache in her heart at seeing him lying there so helpless and fragile.

The doctor and nurses promised to call her immediately if there was any change and told her she could visit again in the morning; assuring her he was progressing fine with good vitals.

"Hey, Craig. You got another hot date tonight? You will have a lot of chaperones if you do." Chase joked trying to ease the tension in the air as they were all escorted inside.

"Not funny, dad." "No way, I will take a girl out with all this militia around."

"Ash, what time does the flight arrive for A. J. and your aunt and uncle?"

"At 8:15 p.m. Director Jones said he would have some agents waiting at the airport to escort them here. A. J. is going to be so confused." Ashley frowned.

"I can't wait to see him and mom and dad." Patrick said while pulling out a chair for Ashley to sit down. "You never realize how important family is to you until you don't have them."

"I hear you." Chase said as he sat down at the table beside them.

Brenda was busy making coffee for everyone as Roberto and Grayson brought in Chase and Ashley's belongings from the hospital.

"Chase, do you think one of the agents could go over to the beach cottage and get some of my things?" Ashley asked.

"Roberto, can you make it happen? I would ask you or Grayson but I am sure neither of you will be more than a sneeze away from us." Chase laughed, still attempting to lighten the air a little bit.

"Ashley, just make us a list of what you need and we will see that it gets here within the hour. And, I will just ignore smart asses sneeze comment for now." Roberto thumped Chase on the head as he walked by him.

Craig popped down on the sofa and turned the TV on and was channel surfing when all channels kept giving the same breaking news story…..

FBI Director Lawrence found dead in his home this evening. It is believed to be suicide. No other details are being released at this time. Stay tuned to the 10 o'clock news report for an update on the story.

"I knew it" Ashley paced the length of the living room again and again, obviously in a lot of pain. She crossed in front of the TV barely looking at it. "I mean -- I didn't know it. I knew there was ….. Something about him. I just thought it would be something else." Her throat went tight, her chest hurt and her eyes burned. "Oh, God, Tony kept saying "No, FBI… No, FBI." He knew, he knew"

Brenda stepped in her path with a cup of coffee in her hands, thrusting it under Ashley's nose. "Settle down, sip this and tell us what you are talking about."

Ashley stopped pacing and glared out the window. Then she looked around.

"It was so… just so odd. I mentioned to Chase that Director Lawrence kept leaving our meetings early and then he stopped us in the parking lot and asked about my relationship with Anthony. He kept referencing he knew me; yet I didn't remember him from anywhere." She looked down into the black liquid in her cup.

'That explains how Tony got burnt!" Chase exclaimed.

"And the silver haired man, the wire transmission from Tony's body microphone….. The silver haired man, Lewis S. Fox; I remember now - he said he owned the director of the FBI! Lawrence is the one that has set us up all along." Ashley said point blank.

"Lewis Fox got away!" Roberto and Grayson both stated in unison.

"That is why my boss Director Madison and Director Jones from CIA were both at the hospital immediately afterwards. That is also why they have taken such lengths to assure our safety. Greg was monitoring the body microphone Tony was wearing and transferred all data; audio and video straight to both of them as it occurred. Director Lawrence knew he was discovered and they would be coming after him, so he killed himself. How the hell did Fox get away?" Chase's brows pulled together, everything made sense now.

"Well, I am glad the bastard killed himself, "I hope it was a slow and painful death. Fox slipped out through that panel door, but they should have apprehended him on the roof." Ashley said. Everyone agreed.

Chase had never seen Ashley the way he saw her then. The way her face changed. The look---yeah, that he recognized. He'd seen that look before---anger, fury, and righteous indignation. In all the years he had known her, he'd never seen this much pure rage. Her walk was even different. Stride, longer. Footfalls, almost stomping. She walked right up to the agent stationed at the back door and tugged the flashlight from his hand. The man swung his head around, mouth open, took one look at her face and snapped it shout again.

Chase thought that was probably a wise decision on his part. Ashley opened the double French doors leading out onto the back patio and shone the light around, as she slammed the door shut. This way, and that way, the light beam moved. It only illuminated the dozen or so agents around the perimeter.

"Damn! How the hell was she going to explain everything she felt to Tony!" She flung the light to the ground, arms rising outward in frustration.

Chase took her shoulders, held on hard. "Take a breath, Ash. Come on, Do it."

She did, but he could see the tears of frustration and fury in her eyes.

"Where are my damn cigarettes?"

Chase opened the door and asked Roberto to check their belongings from the hospital and see if Ash's cigarettes were in any of the stuff.

Roberto returned a few minutes later with her cigarette case.

Ashley snatched out a cigarette, fired it up and drew heavily. She watched the amber glowing end as she exhaled. She really had been trying to quit. Now just wasn't the time.

"You know Chase, all these years we busted our asses, almost died, and spent time away from our families to get low life scum off the street. You know, drug dealers, murderers, rapist, gun dealers, prostitutes, child molesters, etc. My whole outlook on life changed; you know… Guilty until proven innocent. I have seen so many dead bodies that it doesn't even phase me anymore, watched the life slip right out of their bodies with no emotion; now that is sad. And you know why our diligence didn't work? Because, half our elected officials are on the take. I mean, my God! The dirty cops, the medical examiner, the director of the FBI… all owned and in bed with Lewis S. Fox, The Dixie Mafia. And you wonder why I feel that justice is jaded?" Ashley shook her head.

"I know, Ash. It answers a lot of questions I have had for years, you know how, so many times our undercover operations came up just short of the mark. That was because the top hitters knew we were cops, knew we were coming before we even got there!" Chase smiled slightly.

"You know, I am still in love with Anthony." Ashley whispered. "I remember before he left years ago, he had begged me to give it all up. He demanded that I get out of narcotics, to just quit. I wouldn't do it! I was going to make a difference in the world." she sighed with a dejected look.

Chase looked at the door, and then looked at her. "We need to go back inside, I just saw lights come up the driveway, A. J. and your aunt and uncle are probably here."

Ashley ground the cigarette viscously under her shoe and followed Chase back inside his house.

"Momma, Momma." A. J. ran across the room and threw his arms around Ashley's legs.

Ashley kneeled, wincing slightly in pain, to give her son a big hug and kiss.

"We rode on plane, and in big bus. Aunt Lynn let me sit in her lap, but she buckled us both in with one belt. I wanted Leo to come but Uncle Morgan said a horse couldn't ride in plane." A. J.'s excited chatter continued…

Ashley looked across the room at the tears of joy. Aunt Lynn and Uncle Morgan had Patrick engulfed in one big embrace, all three of them crying.

"Thank you, Ashley." Uncle Morgan sobbed.

"Why Aunt Lynn and Uncle Morgan cryin?" A. J. asked, pulling her hand.

"They are happy, honey. They are happy, those are tears of joy." Ashley smiled.

"Why Uncle Chase hopping on one leg? A. J. asked pointing at Chase's leg.

"He hurt his leg, honey."

"He has a boo boo?"

"That's right, your Uncle Chase has a big boo boo, so be careful not to hurt him, okay?" Ashley told her son.

"Okay, momma." A. J. answered, still clinging to his mother's hand, looking up at her bandages around her waist and leg. "Momma, got boo boo's too? Tears began streaking down his little face.

"Yes, honey. But, momma is okay!" Ashley fought back the tears.

"Hey, A. J., wanna go upstairs and see all my new fish?" Craig asked.

"Yea!" A. J. was already running up the stairs

with Craig trailing behind.

Soon everyone was settled in for the night. A. J. was curled up in the bed next to her. Ashley just smiled down at her son, wondering what Anthony would think of him. She called Gina Rae and filled her in on everything and made another quick phone call to the hospital to check on Tony's progress before switching off the bed side lamp and attempting to go to sleep. Shadows danced along the wall from the palms gently blowing near the outside security lights.

CHAPTER NINETEEN

Bright light filtered through the blinds as Ashley lay in bed holding her son. She eased his arms and legs from around her body and slipped out from under the cover, leaving him sleeping soundly.

Thirty minutes later, showered, and changed, somewhat aching; she descended the stairs in search of one of the agents to take her to the hospital.

"Good morning!" Brenda was in the kitchen, and handed her a steaming cup of coffee as she entered.

"Thanks, Brenda. Would you mind making sure A. J. is okay while I visit Tony at the hospital?"

"I would love to! I have missed him so much, he has gotten so big. He can hang out with his Auntie Brenda today."

"Thanks, how is Chase this morning?"

"He had a very bad night, in a lot of pain. He

finally took the pain medicine the doctors gave him at about four a.m. I don't think he will be up for a while." Brenda said.

"Good morning, ladies." Roberto stuck his head around the corner.

"Morning, Roberto can you give me a ride to the hospital? Ashley asked.

"Sure thing. I have been waiting for you to come downstairs. I figured you would want to go first thing this morning." Roberto popped his cell phone out of his pocket and she heard him telling someone to pick them up out front.

Thirty minutes later, Ashley walked down the corridor of the ICU unit and vaguely noticed the Sunday Morning worship services on the T.V.s. Dear God, let him make it through this, Ashley prayed a silent prayer as she entered Anthony's private suite. She approached his bed very quietly and listened to his breathing. His breathing seemed much steadier and his color looked a little better than it did last night. He was still hooked up to several machines and monitors were steadily flashing in the room. She looked over at the monitor showing his heart rate and watched it rhythmically going up and down across the screen and listened as the ventilator pushed air in and out of his lungs. She pulled the chair close to his bed, sat down and took his hand in hers, feeling his warmth. His eyes fluttered slightly.

"Anthony, I know you can't hear me, but I love you so much." Ashley laid her head on the bed next to his shoulder and told him he had a son that looked just like him. "He is four and a half years old, has dark hair and dark eyes that twinkle with mischief, he is so good at playing T-Ball, and he just loves all animals. His name is Anthony John, I named him after you but I call him A. J. ; he is who you heard me on the phone talking to…." Ashley broke off, sobbing softly onto Tony's chest. "I also had cancer almost two years before you left. I went through so many treatments and never told you, I just never could seem to find the right time and once I won the battle and was better, I never had the courage to tell you. I was so worried when I found out that I was pregnant that something would be wrong with our baby because of all the treatments I had went through the year before." Ashley whispered softly to Tony, "A part of me died the day you left and it has never returned to life. The part of you that you gave to me in A. J. is all that has kept me going!" Ashley wiped the tears from her face and rested her cheek on Tony's chest, listening to the labored rise and fall of his heart beating.

Hours later, a nurse came in to check Anthony's vital signs. "Excuse me, ma'am. We have been working around you all day, but we need to assess removing some of the machines now?" the nurse smiled sympathetically at Ashley.

Ashley nodded trying to wake up fully and silently moved from Anthony's bedside, apologizing to the nurse and stepping outside into the corridor.

"How is he?" Roberto asked.

Startled, Ashley spun around. She hadn't seen Roberto sitting in the chair just outside the room.

"He appears to be doing a lot better." Ashley glanced down at her watch. Good Lord, it was 3:00 p.m., she had fallen asleep at his bedside seven hours ago. No wonder the nurse asked her to leave.

"Brenda called earlier to see how you and Tony were doing." "I popped my head in and told her you were sleeping and she said not to disturb you, and to tell you everything was fine there with A. J." Roberto smiled.

"Thanks." Ashley felt a little embarrassed for falling asleep for so long.

"Could I ask you a personal question?" Roberto said.

"Sure." Ashley pressed her lips together.

"I don't mean to pry, but I have been friends with Anthony for fifteen years. Is A. J. his son?" Roberto asked softly.

"Yes, he is. Anthony doesn't know yet." Ashley said looking down at the bleached white tiles.

"I thought so, when I saw him last night. He looks just like his daddy." Roberto said with a huge grin.

The nurse came back out after a couple of hours, wrote some notes on the chart outside the door and went down the corridor and out the double doors.

Ashley stayed until well past dark and Roberto

took her home. They drove home in silence. Ashley played with A.J. for a while, read him a story and put him to bed. She called Gina Rae and gave her an update of everything. Gina answered on the first ring and wanted to get on a plane and fly straight down.

"Ashley. Larry and I have been so worried. We saw A.J. and your aunt and uncle off at the airport. They gave us a brief rundown of what was going on. I am so happy that Patrick is okay, how are you, how bad were you hurt? Gina Rae was speaking so rapidly, Ashley knew she was distraught.

"Hanging in there, barely! I mean I really have no choice right now. A.J. is okay, but so confused. Tony is hurt really bad and still in ICU, they don't know if he will survive. Gina, everything just went south so quickly." Ashley choked back the tears.

"I know, baby. It will all be fine. I am coming down there and you tell Tony he can't kill over yet, I still have to kick his ass!" Gina Rae gave a very strained laugh, attempting to lighten the mood.

"I will be sure to tell him first thing in the

morning, which should bring him out of his coma! I love you, girl." After much talking, Ashley convinced her that it wasn't necessary for her to fly down and promised to call her again tomorrow. She then pulled out her laptop and decided to check her email messages.

Her inbox had several messages but one in particular reached up and grabbed her by the throat in a death grip. It was from FBI Director Lawrence dated two days ago, she slowly opened the email:

To: Agent Ashley Cameron
From: Director Lawrence
Subject: Martinelli Drug Cartel /
Lewis S. Fox – Dixie Mafia

Dear Agent Cameron,
By the time you receive this e-mail I will have reached my demise. It has been a long time coming and I can only relish the end. I regret the pain I have caused my family and the many honest supporters who placed me in a position of trust. I have been on the Adrianno Martinelli

payroll for almost twenty years. This will come as no surprise. But, I was also bought and paid for by the Dixie Mafia. You see, Donna married Fox right out of college against my wishes. So my only daughter was married to the leader of the Dixie Mafia. Lewis S. Fox bought me many years back when my daughter Donna had an affair with a professional boxer at the Mustang Ranch in Reno, Nevada. Fox discovered the affair and went to the Mustang Ranch and murdered the boxer. He was shot six times. He was stabbed twenty six times, once for every year of my daughter's life. A linen handkerchief monogrammed with old English "F" was discovered at the crime scene; shoved down the boxers' throat. The owner of the Mustang Ranch, Forcont was charged but fled extradition to Brazil and is now believed to be in the Cayman Islands. The "F" monogram was not Forcont but Fox. DNA testing can be conducted to prove this element; however it will also contain the DNA of my daughter Donna, placed there by Fox to implicate her. This is what Fox held over my head all these years. If I didn't agree to whatever he wanted, he threatened to have my daughter prosecuted and imprisoned for murder. I have a safe deposit box at First Bay Bank in Bay City, Florida. It contains not only this handkerchief but six flash drives and twelve computer disc which hold all the Martinelli Cartel and Dixie Mafia Financial Records including off shore accounts as well as a Who's Who list of political figures on their payrolls. There is a spreadsheet on the red flash drive which cross references money transfers with contract hits over the past twenty years. You will also find the original autopsies performed by Medical Examiner Sloan that were later falsified. My wife has the key to safety deposit box in her jewelry safe inside a large three inch solid gold locket. She is not aware that the key is there. She and Donna's birth dates are the combination to the safe. Please use extreme caution as it wasn't until five days ago I discovered that the owner of First Bay Bank is also on Lewis Fox's payroll. I knew the first time I met you over ten years ago that you could not be bought and held a high standard of ethics and values. Your adversaries recognized this as well and wished nothing but death upon you, many of them actually took out contracts to facilitate this endeavor over the years. You were luckily, always one step ahead of them. Fox told me once he tried to buy you and you laughed in his face. I trust that you will dispense of this information in a proper and expedited manner. Please assure that my wife and Donna are treated fairly. Donna has suffered greatly at the hands of Fox over the years, and never fully recovered when she gave birth to twin sons, with one dying at birth. Donna has been institutionalized in a mental ward for the past six years. My wife has no knowledge of any of this information regarding the cartel or mafia. I always respected Anthony and waited until the very last minute, until I had no choice; but to out him to Fox. I cannot stress enough for you to be careful; Lewis Fox is slick as hell, as he had the balls to bug my personal office at the FBI. I decided to end things for myself and not give that bastard the pleasure of taking me out as I knew he would. I pray that everyone recovers and can put this nightmare behind them.

Heart of Jaded Justice

Best Regards:

Former FBI Director Lawrence

Ashley stared at the e-mail in disbelief for what seemed an eternity. Two words came to mind, *Jaded Justice*. She forwarded the information immediately to CIA Director Jones and placed one more call to Jones informing him to read the message immediately. She would fill Chase in tomorrow and he could inform his boss. She looked over at the peaceful sleeping figure of her son and thought about his father fighting for his life at the hospital. Director Jones could handle it from here; her first priority for once, was the men in her life.

Ashley was up early the next morning and found Roberto waiting to take her back to the hospital.

Ashley was surprised when she re-entered Anthony's room to find him awake, with only a few tubes and monitors remaining. The doctor was just leaving the room and said his progress was miraculous and simply unexplainable.

Anthony couldn't take his eyes off her. She was

wearing tight fitting jeans and a mint green tank top, one that bared her delectable shoulders. Tony's gut tied itself in knots. He wanted to kiss the exposed skin until she trembled. Damn! He had been on deaths door and this was all he could awaken too…

Ashley stared at him in silence for what seemed an eternity. He looked tormented. He turned away from her suddenly and stared out the window.

Still not looking at her, he finally said, "I don't deserve a second chance, but I don't think I can just let you walk out of my life again."

Ashley's heart thumped unsteadily. She wanted to go to him, to take him in her arms and promise never to leave, but she forced herself to stay where she was; he was the one that left her over five years ago, she wasn't the one that walked; he was.

"Why?" she asked. "What is different now, you left without a glance backwards almost six years ago."

A very dry almost chuckle escaped his parched lips. "You think I just ran away. Let me explain something Ashley and if you want to leave, I won't try to stop you." Anthony said solemnly.

She nodded, sitting down in the chair beside his bed.

"Six years ago, I asked you to give up your career with no explanations. The Martinelli Cartel was coming after you. You had two contracts out on your life. I went to work with the CIA and we took out both killers before they could get to you. I knew they would just send others. It goes back a little further...." He hesitated his voice cracking.

"What are you talking about?" she asked, puzzled.

"The night at the Martinelli Mansion, the night the two agents, got killed and you nearly died.... He met her gaze, swallowed hard, and then tried again. "I am the one that tripped the guide wire that set off the explosion. I was coming across the lawn toward you and never saw it... Until it was too late.." the words were ripped from his tortured soul. "I caused the death of other cops and almost killed the woman I love. I had just received the radio transmission that the SWAT team was under ambush and was trying to get you to pull back!"

"Oh, my God!" Ashley exclaimed. "That's why you left?"

"I hurt you, almost got you killed, caused the death of two good agents. I am so sorry." "I left here and went deep undercover, vowing to take down the Martinelli Cartel so they could never hurt you or anyone else again." he said, turning back to her.

She just stared at him.

"I can't live without you, Ashley." he choked out. "I tried, for six damn years almost, and it didn't work. I need you with me, sweetheart."

A single tear slid down her cheek. He instantly reached over and brushed it away, his touch so gentle she only began to cry harder.

Remorse flooded his gaze. "All the time we lost." He said simply.

"I was wrong." she whispered.

"We both were," he corrected. His dark eyes darkened.

"I should never have left you, baby. I should

have told you the truth and we could have faced it all together." Anthony's voice was weak with past regrets and current physical pain.

Sliding closer, Ashley crawled gently up on the bed; Tony wrapped his good arm around her waist. He lifted his hand to stroke her hair. He pushed a few wayward strands away from her face, and then his mouth came down on hers. The kiss sent a thrill through her body, sizzling down her spine and settling deep inside of her. When his tongue licked at her lips, she whimpered, opening her mouth to grant him access. His tongue slid inside, dueling with hers, exploring every crevice.

When they finally broke apart, they were both panting; both hurting from their recent injuries, but reluctant to put any distance between them.

Ashley drug her finger along the line of his jaw, and gently across the bandaging around his neck; smiling again. "I have something else to tell you, Tony."

It took a second for his brain to function again.

"You have a four and a half year old son. His name is Anthony John, A. J. for short." She said breathlessly, afraid to look at him.

Anthony closed his eyes for what seemed an eternity. Once he reopened them; small tears slid down his face.

"I remember you telling me yesterday, I was in and out of it.... But I could hear you very far away. I thought I was dreaming one of the best dreams I had ever had." "When can I meet him?" Anthony's voice was raspy with emotion.

"As soon as you get out of here, Aunt Lynn and Uncle Morgan flew in with him Saturday night. They were watching him while I came here to work." she had tears in her eyes.

"What day is it anyway?" Tony asked confused.

"It is Monday morning. You have been in the unit since Friday night when all hell broke loose." Ashley grimaced.

"You really had cancer too didn't you?" He asked with tears in his eyes.

She childishly kept her gaze on the floor not wanting to look at him, afraid he would see her in a lesser way.

"Look at me," he said. When she refused he cupped her chin with both hands and forced the eye contact. The movement causing him physical pain.

"Yes, I did." she muttered, unable to stop the pain that seeped into her tone.

"I'm sorry, sorry you didn't tell me, sorry I didn't recognize how sick you were… Why didn't you tell me?" His dark eyes glittered with remorse.

"I didn't want to see pity in your eyes, I wanted you home because you loved me and wanted to be there. All you did back then was stay gone and come home drunk." Ashley said barely a whisper.

A tear slid down her cheek. He brushed it away with his thumb, his touch infinitely gently and unbelievably warm.

"I was an awful man in a lot of ways, but if you give me another chance, I will never leave your side. What does my son look like?" Anthony asked, barely a whisper.

"Look in the mirror. He looks just like you!"

Ashley smiled, finally fully meeting his gaze.

His smile widened, revealing his perfectly straight white teeth. "I will never leave your side again, Ashley, I mean it. In fact, I think we should get married. Right now!"

She grinned. "Oh, really? Right here in the hospital?"

He shot her a roguish look. "I did propose the first night we met, and you said yes. There's not a statute of limitations on proposals. So since you said yes the first time around, it still stands." His voice was thick.

"Okay, you do know we were both drunk the first night we met, right?" Ashley laughed then sobered quickly, "Just promise me one thing. Wherever your job takes us, wherever my job takes us; just promise you'll never leave my side, baby. We stay together for better or worse. We talk everything out and don't let anything come between us." Her heart skipped a beat when she breathlessly finished.

He smiled faintly, tiring easily. "Just one more thing from me. I want to tell you I love you."

A rush of heat seared her entire body. That she was able to breathe normally was nothing short of a miracle.

"I'm not sure you heard me. Should I say it again?" he teased quietly.

She nodded.

"I love you." He dipped his head and pressed a tender kiss to her lips. "I love you, Ashley. I will spend the rest of my life proving to you just how much!"

Finally, regaining the capacity for speech, she met his gaze; her voice heavy with emotion. "I love you, too…. Anthony."

All the emotion and trying to talk too much had worn Anthony out quickly. Ashley stayed for hours and watched him sleep. Nurses continued to come in and out throughout the day and he seemed to be progressing greatly and healing more rapidly than they could fathom.

It was late evening; a beautiful orange sunset was glowing as it set lazily on the horizon.

Anthony was so exhausted and weak; he again drifted off to sleep like a baby. For the first time, in a very long time; the smile on his face reached deep into his heart and soul.

Ashley would fill him in on FBI Director Lawrence later, right now she just watched him sleep.

EPILOGUE

Ten Months Later

"Ashley, are you out here?" Tony tossed the mail on the bar and strode outside searching the private stretch of warm, white sand for his wife. He spotted her sitting on an oversize towel a few yards away, shielded by a colorful pink-and-green umbrella and sipping on a glass of wine.

Where was A.J.? He shielded his eyes and spotted him running up and down the beach, chasing his German shepherd puppy. Leo was a beautiful black and tan shepherd and was the first present he had bought his son, ten months earlier. At a year old, Leo still hadn't outgrown his chewing stage; especially shoes. Lately, he had turned into a thief as well; stealing toys, food, keys, mail, and pretty much anything he could get his mouth on. They knew to search his dog bed for anything that went missing.

He had just gotten in from St. Andrews, and broken every traffic law in order to get to the beach house they'd bought eight months earlier, two months after his full release from the hospital rehab unit. Ashley had left a cryptic message on his voicemail, something about a change of plans. He'd immediately picked up on the note of anxiety in her voice, so he bid goodbye to his team at the airstrip and rushed home like a maniac. And what did he find? His wife is relaxing on the beach; A. J. and Leo chasing waves.

"What's going on, Mrs. Langston?" he demanded as he reached her towel.

The sun set high in the middle of the clear blue sky. It was bright as hell, and Tony was squinting through his dark sunshades as she tilted her head up at him. Her face was tanned and radiant; her body covered by a green bikini that rose high with little strings on each side of her thighs and barely covered her breasts.

They'd been living in Costa Rica for eight months now, though the beach house in St. Andrews they were given was their real home base, it was where they were married nine months ago. Now that was a site; both he and Ashley hobbling down the aisle to say their I do's... the whole wedding party looked like world war survivors, some still in casts and bandages. Gina Rae and Larry had to push wheelchairs and assist those with walking canes to their seats. Uncle Morgan had given her away. She stood beside her two maids of honor; Gina Rae and Brenda, just as Tony had two best men; Chase and Larry. The ceremony was simply and magnificent at the same time. Director Madison and Director Jones had bought their old cottage and given it to them as a wedding present. They came and went with caution as the silver fox was still on the loose. Ashley had given Gina Rae and Larry part ownership in Cameron Investigations and handled the business from either Bay City or the beach house here. Gina Rae had accused her of using the gift as a bribe to keep her from killing Tony before she could marry him.

    Despite all their traveling they kept up with what was going on in the states. The most recent news had been the downfall of the Dixie Mafia. They had enough information on Lewis Fox to secure indictments for several murders and would again be using the RICO Act. The government had already begun seizing properties and assets which, Fox had obtained through his racketeering activities. So far, Fox was in hiding. They had arrested numerous political figures based on the information in Lawrence safe deposit box, including the owner of the bank.

"Why do you look so worried?" she asked, setting down her glass on the rickety little table she'd dragged out onto the beach their first day there.

"Because of you." he said darkly. "What was that message about? Change of plans? What on earth are you talking about?"

She gave a shrug, "I just wanted to let you know we might need to alter some of the plans we made for this month."

"Such as?" he asked.

"You can't go to Mexico." The dimple in her chin appeared.

Tony frowned. "Why do I need to cancel Mexico?"

Another innocent little shrug. "You have a birthday, and the whole gang is flying out here for a week."

His heart started beating normal with relief.

Ashley grinned. "Got you!"

He couldn't help but laugh. "I should've known. Roberto and Grayson were acting all weird, so were Chase and Brenda when I stopped by their house. They send their best. I picked up our mail from St. Andrews and put it on the bar inside."

Ashley's eyes twinkled. "It will be the best party you have ever known. The whole gang is coming; Chase, Brenda and Craig, Roberto and his family, Grayson and his family, Geek Boy Greg and his girlfriend, Gina Rae and Larry, Director Madison and Director Jones and their families, Aunt Lynn and Uncle Morgan and Patrick and… Oh yeah, I forgot to tell you, Patrick is engaged…..to the CIA Agent that supervised his witness protection."

Tony's heart squeezed with emotion. After everything that had happened to them both; it was an easy assumption that the change of plans meant bad news. He was happy to be wrong.

"Daddy, daddy, daddy; you're home! A. J. ran up and grabbed Tony by the leg, followed by Leo, kicking sand up everywhere and barking ferociously.

"How's my little man today?" Tony effortlessly lifted A. J. in the air and began twirling him around and around.

"Good, daddy." A. J.'s excited giggles filled the air.

Ashley laughed and beckoned them to sit down next to her on the sandy beach. It felt so good having the two best men in her life at her side.

With a grin, he sank onto the sand, still holding A.J. on one side, while wrapping his other arm around his gorgeous wife. They stared out across the emerald ocean waters noting in particular where everything met the horizon. As their lips met, he knew without a doubt that he'd finally found what he'd been yearning for his entire life. Trust, Love, Happiness, and above all Family.

They were still sitting there in each other's

embrace hours later as the golden embers of the sunset cast its magical glow across the waters on the horizon. A. J. and Leo had found a flock of seagulls and were chasing them up and down the beach, life didn't get any better. In the sun, their scars had faded and the nightmares were seldom. Their days were filled with air fragrant of clean salt water and nights of gently breezes from old palm trees.

Neither Ashley nor Tony knew that inside on the bar; lay a small package with no return address. Its contents......
A linen handkerchief with a bright red old English "F" monogrammed dead center.....

Heart of Jaded Justice

ACKNOWLEDGEMENTS

I would first like to THANK YOU for reading my first novel. It has truly been a pleasure to write and I look forward to bringing many more to you in the near future.

There are no words thankful enough to express my appreciation to Stephanie and Judy at the Times for assisting with proofing and editing; to Suzanne for being the little sister I never had and sharing a common dream to write; to Katie, Carey, and Becky for being my first readers and encouraging me to proceed; to Regina for truly being my rock and best friend throughout the years, working with me to provide a unique cover design and fighting with me over the photo headshots.

Thank you to my mother for sharing her love of reading and always believing I could do anything; my sister and brother-in-law for simply always being there and keeping me grounded when I headed for left field;

and to my daughter for being a trooper while growing up and relocating very often out of necessity and for blessing me with three beautiful grandbabies.

This book is dedicated to my Father; thank you dad for living your life as an inspiration to me and all whom had the privilege of knowing you. I miss you!

Special thanks to Nanna Mae for never being judgmental, always loving and believing in me no matter what; and to Cowboy and Mac for being the best Cops I ever knew and teaching me everything you could. Last, but certainly not least; thanks to Belladonna, my four legged baby for resting at my feet hours on end, night after night as I wrote "Heart of Jaded Justice."

ABOUT THE AUTHOR

R. L. Dodson grew up in southern Alabama and holds a B.S. in History and Criminal Justice. She has spent almost twenty years working in the Criminal Justice Arena. From an early age, she loved to read and later wrote poetry and short stories. This is her first novel and she hopes that you enjoy taking this journey with her. When she is not working, she enjoys writing, oil painting, spending time with her grandchildren and her pit-bull Belladonna and her hound-dog Bubba. R. L. now resides in Florida.

R. L. loves to hear from her readers.
Visit her at:
rl.dodson@yahoo.com
https:www.facebook.com/RLDodsonAuthor
https://twitter.com/RLDodson1

Coming Soon

Crossroads
of
Jaded
Justice

R. L. Dodson

Made in the USA
San Bernardino, CA
05 March 2013